touching snow

m. sindy felin

atheneum books for young readers

new york london toronto sydney

FOR MY MOTHER,
IMMACULEE ANTOINETTE FRANÇOIS DENIS

ATHENEUM BOOKS FOR YOUNG READERS
An imprint of Simon & Schuster Children's Publishing Division
1230 Avenue of the Americas, New York, New York 10020
This book is a work of fiction. Any references to historical events, real people,
or real locales are used fictitiously. Other names, characters, places, and
incidents are products of the author's imagination, and any resemblance to
actual events or locales or persons, living or dead, is entirely coincidental.
Copyright © 2007 by M. Sindy Felin ▪ All rights reserved,
including the right of reproduction in whole or in part in any form.
ATHENEUM BOOKS FOR YOUNG READERS
is a registered trademark of Simon & Schuster, Inc.
For information about special discounts for bulk purchases, please
contact Simon & Schuster Special Sales at 1-866-506-1949 or
business@simonandschuster.com. ▪ The Simon & Schuster Speakers
Bureau can bring authors to your live event. For more information or
to book an event, contact the Simon & Schuster Speakers Bureau at
1-866-248-3049 or visit our website at www.simonspeakers.com.
Also available in an Atheneum Books for Young Readers hardcover edition
Book design by Michael McCartney. ▪ The text for this book is set in Bodoni.
Manufactured in the United States of America
First Atheneum Books for Young Readers paperback edition March 2011
2 4 6 8 10 9 7 5 3 1
The Library of Congress has cataloged the hardcover edition as follows:
Felin, M. Sindy. ▪ Touching snow / M. Sindy Felin. –1st ed.
p. cm. ▪ Summary: After her stepfather is arrested for child abuse,
thirteen-year-old Karina's home life improves, but while the severity of
her older sister's injuries and the urging of her young sister, their uncle,
and a friend tempt her to testify against him, her mother and other
well-meaning adults persuade her to claim responsibility.
ISBN 978-1-4169-1795-3 (hc) ▪ [1. Child abuse—Fiction.
2. Family problems—Fiction. 3. Haitian Americans—Fiction.
4. Stepfathers—Fiction. 5. New York (State)—Fiction.] I. Title.
PZ7.F33579 Tou 2007 ▪ [Fic]—dc22 ▪ 2006014794
ISBN 978-1-4424-1735-9 (pbk) ▪ ISBN 978-1-4424-1736-6 (eBook)

ACKNOWLEDGMENTS

———

Thanks to Jennifer Repo whose initial interest in what was little more than a few pages and an idea encouraged me to finish this story. Many thanks to my agent, Barbara Markowitz, for her honesty and enthusiasm. To my first readers—Scarlett K. Anderson, Kervens Dor, and Cree Pierre—thank you for your feedback. Special thanks to my brother, J. Phillip François, and my stepfather, Dameus Denis, for helping me brush up on my French and Creole.

Finally, my deepest and most profuse thanks go to my editor, Jordan Brown, for his countless hours of work on draft after draft, his devotion to these characters, and his incredible sense of story.

1.

The best way to avoid being picked on by high school bullies is to kill someone. Anyone will do. Accidental killings have the same effect as on-purpose murder. Of course, this is just my own theory. My sister Delta would say that my sample size isn't big enough to draw such a conclusion. But I bet I'm right.

Because now no one jerks my braids so my neck snaps back and I bite my tongue; no one pulls my backpack off and scatters my textbooks in one hallway, my notebooks in another, and leaves the bag in the boys' bathroom toilet; no one spits at me from the school bus; and Gorilla Arms Manning doesn't pretend to point with his right hand while grabbing my crotch with his left. Not since eighth grade. Not since I killed the Daddy.

He wasn't my real daddy. My sisters and I had to call him that when our little brothers were born so they would know what to call him. Before that I just called him Umm. Like "Umm . . . remember you said you would let us watch TV this weekend?" Or "Umm . . . do you want any more rice and plantains?" That's because Ma never told us what our name for him was.

A couple days after my fifth birthday Ma returned to the apartment we shared with Uncle Andre and Aunt Jacqueline and three of my cousins, and made my sisters and me put on matching pink-and-white girly dress-up dresses—the kind with the frilly decorations that scratch your neck and the giant bows in back that never tie to quite the same size, so you end up looking like a crippled-winged angel. Then we went to a church and there was a wedding and we moved out of Brooklyn to a red and yellow house in a place full of white folks called Chestnut Valley and never went back to Uncle Andre's apartment. Ma called her new husband Gaston. But my sister Enid got slapped when she tried that.

The Daddy was only a shade lighter than black as dirt. According to Ma, there are two ways to be considered black as dirt. Your skin could really be black as dirt, or you could be any shade darker than Ma and piss her off. Since Ma is the color of Haitian eggnog, as light all over as the palm of my hand, and since it's almost impossible not to piss her off, most people, including all us kids, are from time to time black as dirt.

But the Daddy was honest-to-goodness almost black as dirt. And so fat he spent most of his time tugging his pants up. Augustin, who worked as a tailor and lived in our basement, made him a few pairs of pants. Tents, they were, really. Tents with crotches sewn into them. My little brother Gerald once suggested it would be easier if the Daddy wore a dress, like one of those big, no-shape, huge-pockets-on-the-side dresses my aunts had to wear after living in New York for a few months.

We all were afraid the mark the Daddy's fist left on Gerald's mouth would forever be black as dirt, but sure enough, it went to purple, then green, then yellow, and back to normal red pink again.

Daddy-black-as-dirt-and-too-fat-for-his-pants had two things my mother liked. He had a desire to live in houses with backyards, houses with white people next door, houses nowhere near subways or bars on school windows or around corners from thieves who stuck knives to your throat and took your money as soon as you stepped out of the bodega/pharmacy/check-cashing store. And he had no wife.

Daddy-black-as-dirt didn't want most of what Ma had—three fatherless daughters, plus four sisters, two brothers, twelve nieces, and seven nephews waiting patiently and hungrily just outside of Port-au-Prince for their chance to come to America—"the great country of New York," they called it—and touch snow. But Ma did have a green card and skin the color of *kremas*, so they married.

I can tell you the whole story about how the Daddy died, if you'd like to hear it, but don't think you'll turn me in. No one would believe you. What the kids at school are saying are only rumors, high school gossip. Maybe it started because of something I whispered to Gorilla Arms Manning the very last time he cornered me at my locker. I don't know. But anyway, I was only fourteen and the Daddy was mean. I have the pictures to prove it. I'll say it was self-defense. Or I suffered psychological trauma. Or maybe I'll just sit there while the cops and the shrinks try to question me and say nothing at all.

Before I start, though, let me ask, you do understand English pretty well, right?

You have to understand, I didn't just up and decide to kill him one day. It's just that 1986 turned out to be quite a year, with Enid almost getting killed and then me meeting Rachael Levinson and then the whole thing with the Daddy. That was only a couple years ago now, but I'm darn sure there are lots of other people in Chestnut Valley, New York, who won't be forgetting that year either for a long time. I guess if I had to pinpoint exactly when it all began, I'd say it was the last day of seventh grade. That was the day Mrs. Mahajan told me if my grades and behavior didn't improve in eighth grade, she'd recommend to the high school guidance counselors that I be placed in learning-disabled classes.

At first, everything was going okay that last day of school. We spent most of the day preparing the classroom for the following year's seventh graders. My sister Delta would be in Mrs. Mahajan's class. Delta is two years younger than me, but ever since Miss Smartypants skipped the third grade, she had always gotten the same teacher I had the year before. It really sucked for her because they always called her Karina practically until Halloween or Thanksgiving. Delta and I look alike in the face and everything, but she's a total shrimp, only half my size. I think the teachers did that on purpose so they'd have one less name to remember when school started. Delta said the teachers did it because I was the weirdest kid they'd ever had in a class and they'd have nightmarish flashbacks when they looked at her. That wasn't a very nice thing for Delta to say. I mean, I admit I'm not a teacher butt kisser like Delta, and I have . . . you know, *moments*, but I don't think I'm so weird.

There were only a couple hours left to the day when we'd finished cleaning up the classroom. Mrs. M. assigned us a one-page essay: "How I Plan on Making My Summer Vacation Productive." She said she wanted us to read it out loud so we could get ideas from one another on how to keep our minds active and incorporate our seventh-grade lessons into our summer learning experiences. What a crock. Like we'd go brain-dead from three months in the sun unless we turned every little thing we did into a learning experience?

The only learning experience I'd ever had over a summer vacation was when I got bored and taught myself the alphabet in sign language. I learned it from the encyclopedia. And the one time I incorporated it into the summer was on a drive to Brooklyn to visit my cousins. I signed H-E-L-P M-E and C-A-L-L P-O-L-I-C-E over and over again out the back window. Right after we passed through the George Washington Bridge toll-booth, the lady in the car next to ours started slapping her husband's shoulder and pointing at me. Then she started making all these crazy signals with her hands. I freaked out. I slid down in the seat and put my head in Enid's lap. Enid licked her fingertips and smoothed down the hair at my temples. "What kinda stories are you dreaming up now, Katu?" she asked me. I ignored her and concentrated on stopping the pounding in my chest. Finally I thought I should get up and sign J-U-S-T K-I-D-D-I-N-G, but by the time I did, the crazy lady's car was gone. I spent the rest of the summer expecting cops to show up at our house, but they never did.

Anyway, that September I had the best "What I Did on My Summer Vacation" essay. I made up a sad story about finally being able to communicate with my lonely, retarded deaf cousins and their poor, sweet deaf parents. I threw in a bit about finding a boy lost in Coney Island, surrounded by useless people who couldn't make out his frantic hand gestures, and how I managed to interpret what he was signing and lead him back into the embrace of his grateful and weeping mother. The kids in my class sat drop jawed. Jay Rosenthal's trip to an Israeli kibbutz and Renee Zondervan's campout at the Grand Canyon couldn't compete; they did that every year. Even my teacher was impressed. I left out the part about pretending to be a kidnapping victim.

This afternoon in Mrs. Mahajan's class I wanted to make up a story about planning to visit Disney World. But most of the kids in my class had already been there. I'd have to do research to make my September essay believable to them, and I wasn't about to give myself a summerlong homework assignment.

For a split second I actually thought of writing the truth. How I planned on spending the entire summer, like every other summer, cooped up on Fairview

Avenue. And it wasn't even the whole darn block, to be really honest. It was just as far as Ma could see from our front yard. That meant we could roller skate between Alaska Street—where the convenience store and the neighborhood pervert Mr. Hollings's house were—and Ridge Lane. Ridge Lane was at the top of the Fairview Avenue hill, and we weren't allowed to cross it because then we'd be on the other side and out of sight. Once, we spent the entire summer in the backyard because somebody was going around snatching little black children off the streets of Atlanta. Ma said a person that crazy probably wouldn't even bother to find out that we were Haitian and not black, and he would snatch us, too. I thought of explaining to her that Atlanta wasn't in any part of New York, but then I figured what's the use. When I'd tried to tell her Chicago wasn't a different country, she'd still spent a whole month and a half getting us all passports to go to my uncle's wedding.

I ended up not having to do the stupid essay, though, because right after she assigned it, Mrs. Mahajan called me to her desk.

"The middle school teachers will be having their annual meeting with high school counselors at the beginning of next semester," she said.

Mrs. Mahajan had a perfectly round, pencil-eraser-size red dot sitting between her eyebrows. It was red because the flowers on her sari were red. The day before her sari was mostly yellow and so was her dot. The dot doesn't move. Even when her eyebrows are twitching—

one going up and the other moving sideways at the same time.

"Do you know what that means, Karina?" she twitched.

By this time most of the kids had stopped working on their essays and were listening to me get chewed out. I shrugged and silently repeated my name the way Mrs. M. pronounced it, rolling the *r* as if she were Puerto Rican: Ka-*rrr*-ina, Ka-*rrr*-ina, Ka-*rrr*-ina. I crossed my eyes hard until I could see the tip of my nose, then raised my head slightly and watched two red dots bounce across Mrs. M.'s forehead.

"We will be discussing track placement for all of the following year's ninth graders," her two mouths said in unison. "I'm not so sure at the rate you're going you could handle work at even the below-track pace."

"Ooooh!" cried someone from the back of the room.

Then the entire class erupted into laughter. I was so used to hearing kids laugh at me I didn't bother turning around to see who had started it all this time. I crossed my arms and yawned. Mrs. Mahajan took off her glasses, and I stepped to the side to let her give the class her best evil eye.

"That's enough," said Mrs. M. The laughter turned to giggling and hushed snorts.

I thought she had to be kidding about the below-average classes. Sure, my grades weren't great. But that was because Mrs. M. put so much weight on homework. That had never been my particular strength, but I did just fine on all my tests. That should count more than doing work at home, where you could get your older brother or sister to do it, right? Anyway, I thought placements were made using the Iowa standardized tests we took every year. That year the test results had shown me reading at the college-sophomore level, same as Delta. My mom called all our relatives and hung the results on the refrigerator door. I thought college sophomores must be pretty dumb, but I kept that to myself.

"Ka-*rrr*-ina?"

Mrs. Mahajan waited for me to respond. I uncrossed my eyes and let out a breath hard enough to flutter the stiff scarf teetering on her head like a half-closed umbrella. Mrs. M. let out a breath of her own, then smoothed out a copy of my report card with both her bony hands.

"Considering these grades and considering your incorrigible attitude, perhaps the best placement for you would be in a special-education class," she said.

Bang! Just like that she went from putting me in below-average classes to classes with retards! I couldn't believe what I was hearing. Over and over again Ma had warned that something like this might happen to me. With every bad report card I took home, she'd remind me that she had to work as hard as she did because she didn't have an education. "In New York if you have a high school diploma, you work at a sit-behind-a-desk job," she'd say while licks of the Daddy's belt sliced my back. "I didn't come to this country to kill myself in the factory just so you could join me there!" And Gorilla Arms Manning was in the retard class. It was bad enough I was the weird kid in school, but now on top of that Jeffrey "Gorilla Arms" Manning and his friends wouldn't even have to wait until recess or lunch to kick the crap out of me every day.

I don't remember how I got back to my seat after Mrs. M. handed me my report card. I remember I could hardly breathe when I sat down at my desk in square five, at the back of the class. And I remember thinking something bad was probably going to happen pretty soon.

The only good thing about being in Mrs. Mahajan's class that year was that Suzanne Ryan and I sat in the same square, our desks right next to each other. And the worst thing about being in Mrs. Mahajan's class was that David Pelletier sat on the other side of Suzanne.

The only ones who weren't still laughing at me were Suzanne and David. David was giving her this notebook-paper-wrapped Happy Summer Vacation present, and Suzanne was pretending to be so happy about it, even though she hadn't opened it yet. You know, like when adults tell you to say thank you for a birthday present even before you open it, so maybe you're saying thank you for a really crappy present? Like that, only Suzanne was also making these lovey eyes at him. It was gross.

I thought Suzanne was the prettiest girl in the school. She had these sparkly braces on her teeth, and the tip of her nose and two little spots on her cheeks were always red. But she didn't wear makeup. They were just like that. And her hair was so shiny blond it was practically white. Her lips were the coolest, though. They were always pink and shiny. She wore bubble-gum-smelling lip gloss that came out of a little tiny jar, not a tube like regular Chap Stick. And when she put on the lip gloss, she used her middle finger instead of her index finger, and she put her lips way up in the air into an O. It seemed to me her lips were always in that O.

Like when I told her earlier that year that my grades had improved, and she said, "Oh, Karina, no they didn't. Three Ds and a C last report card, and three Ds and a C this report card."

I pointed to the rest of the report card, where you get marks for being at school on time and behaving well with others and following instructions and all that stuff. I had gone from mostly twos and threes to almost all ones and a couple of twos.

Suzanne said, "Oh, number grades don't count, Karina, because we're almost in high school. You should know that."

Well, I did know that then, and even though we had had that conversation, like, two report cards ago, I really wanted to let her know right now that I knew that. But Suzanne had her back to me, making goo-goo noises at David. Her hair was lying on her back, not in a ponytail like usual, and I thought maybe if I could just touch her hair and smell her bubble-gum lips, I could breathe again and Mrs. Mahajan and the high school counselors wouldn't put me in the retarded class with Gorilla Arms and then Ma wouldn't be so ashamed she'd have to give me a beat-up and maybe I could be like all the other kids and wear shorts to school on hot days and have best friends and get notebook-paper-wrapped Happy Summer Vacation, See You Next Year presents.

I must have started breathing okay again, because next thing I knew, Suzanne and I were rolling around the floor, and she was screaming and kicking at me. I looked up when I heard Mrs. Mahajan yell, "Let her go! Let her go!" I looked to where Mrs. M. was pointing and saw Suzanne's white blond hair twisted around my fist.

Have you ever heard Enid call me the fainting queen? Well, she used to. I don't know why it happens, exactly. Sometimes when I get real upset or nervous, I try to pretend I'm someplace else, then *boom!*—suddenly I'm on the floor wigging out. Mr. Cohen tried to talk to Ma about it once, but she told him that I was faking it. I don't think he believed her, though.

When Mrs. M. sent me to Mr. Cohen that afternoon, I was actually really glad to go. Mr. Cohen was a very nice principal and a really good listener even though his ears were full of hair. He wasn't like the principal we have now at the high school, who stands in the hallway, clasping his hands behind his back, rocking back and forth on his heels and giving everyone the evil eye.

There was a purple chair right outside Mr. Cohen's office. Next to it was a red chair. The red chair was where you sat before you got called into his office. The purple chair was for afterward, when he sent you back out for some quiet time to yourself. I didn't get a chance to sit in the red chair that day. Mr. Cohen was standing at the door waiting for me.

"The problem this time, Karina. What would it seem to be?" Mr. Cohen talked funny that way, and real slow, too. That's because he didn't learn to speak English until he came to New York straight from a concentration camp, and he was, like, ninety years old. David Pelletier said that Mr. Cohen was so hungry when he was at the concentration camp that he'd had to eat dirt and bugs. And he said that Mr. Cohen always wore long sleeves so no one would see the numbers the Nazis tattooed on his arm. But I think he wore long shirts because old people are always cold. My grandmother is. Even if it's summer, no matter if she is inside or out, it's long sleeves and sweaters. And I know she doesn't have any Nazi tattoos.

"I couldn't breathe," I said.

"Breathing now. It's good?"

"Yeah." I panted a little to show him.

"Maybe next time you raise your hand, like this, to tell teacher you can't breathe?"

I raised my hand too. "That's a good idea," I said.

Mr. Cohen suggested I go out to the purple chair to practice raising my hand and think about not attacking my fellow students whenever I'm short of breath. I didn't move.

"There is more?" he asked.

I wanted to come right out and tell him how unfair Mrs. Mahajan was being, making plans to send me to special ed just because I didn't always do my homework. I wanted to ask him what was so educational about clothes hanger collages depicting the destruction of the environment or shoe box replicas of the solar system, anyway. I wanted to tell him about the things that usually kept me busy at home after school, the things we weren't allowed to tell anybody, especially white people. And I would have told him all that, plus how my mom would feel like a failure if I ended up packing boxes at the factory, but instead I cried.

Don't think I'm a sissy or anything, because I'm totally not. It was just turning out to be a very, very bad last day of a very bad school year. And Mr. Cohen, being the nice concentration-camp-survivor type of guy he was, wasn't going to write my mother a note about my behavior on the last day of school so that I'd start my summer vacation with a beat-up. Not especially if I cried.

Now, my summer and the beginning of the next semester would be even worse than seventh grade, and it would start with the Daddy that very afternoon, but Mr. Cohen didn't know that, and I didn't know it then either.

"Is this because of the special-education class?" Mr. Cohen asked after watching me cry for a while. I should have guessed he already knew. Mr. Cohen was the boss of the middle school. He knew everything.

I nodded. Then my crying turned into hiccuping, and not being able to keep my mouth closed made me drool onto my jeans, and that made me cry even louder.

"Oy, okay, okay. Oy, okay," said Mr. Cohen.

He put his hand on my back and led me out to the purple chair. "Sit and think how to stay out of special education, Karina. No more class for you today."

Mr. Cohen left me alone in the hallway and returned to his office.

I wanted to make a to-do list for staying out of special ed and put on it things like "Do homework every single night" and "Do all extra-credit assignments" and stuff like that, but all I could think of right then was that if I wasn't going to be allowed back in class, it would be three months before I saw Suzanne again. That wasn't fair. I wanted to say sorry for grabbing her, and besides, I had my own Happy Summer Vacation, See You Next Year present to give to her. I hadn't thought of using notebook paper to wrap it in, though. It was just sitting at the bottom of my backpack.

As soon as the end-of-school bell rang, I ran into the classroom and grabbed my bag. Mrs. M. was there alone. She called my name, but I ignored her and ran out to the buses. Suzanne was just about to board the number 23 when I called her name. When she saw me coming, she grabbed her head and started backing away.

"I'm not gonna do it again, Suzanne. That was an accident before."

"Oh God, Karina, you say that every time."

David walked by with his best friend, Bobby L., and fake sneezed "Freak!" into his hands. Bobby L. nearly snotted all over the place laughing, then pretended to accidentally bump into David, who then shoved me into the side of the bus. I didn't even fall. I'd gotten real good by then at bracing myself when those morons were around. I just rolled my eyes and turned back to Suzanne.

"I have something for you," I said, and pulled a brand-new jumbo-size pink and silver pen out of my backpack. Hanging from the cap was a string of purple yarn tied into a loop large enough to hang the pen around your neck.

"I don't want it," Suzanne said. But she said it while she was staring real hard at the pen, so I knew she was lying.

"Check this out," I said, and scribbled onto my palm. "It writes in silver glitter."

"Oh, so *what*?"

I shrugged. "I thought it was cool."

Suzanne let go of her head and took the pen from me.

"What's this?" She pulled out the folded piece of paper I had stuck underneath the pen's clip.

"It's my address. You can use the pen to write me letters over summer vacation, and I'll write you back. What's your address?"

Suzanne didn't look at me. She was really into the jumbo glitter pen, so I said, "That's okay, I'll get your address from the envelope when you write."

I thought maybe I should hug Suzanne good-bye, and I even saw myself doing it and giving her air kisses and rocking back and forth and saying, "I'm gonna miss you sooooo much!" like the girls always do to one another on the last day of school. Instead I took a great big step back away from her. I knew what happens when I start to imagine things; without me even knowing it, I'm suddenly doing for real what I saw in my mind, and then girls are screaming and kicking me.

I didn't need that again.

2.

Enid was already at home because high school let out at two o'clock. She opened the front door before Delta and I had a chance to ring the bell, and handed Roland to me.

"Change his diapers and then wash your hands," she ordered. "Dee Dee, you set the table."

Enid acted like she was the boss of everyone when there were no adults at home. Well, technically she was the boss, since she was the oldest, but she didn't have to act like she liked it so much.

I put Roland down on the floor and took my sweet time taking off my backpack. Gerald came hobbling out of the bathroom and hugged my legs. Before I could bend down to kiss his forehead, he let go and hurled himself into Delta. They both fell to the floor laughing.

"What happened to Gerald's braces?" I asked. Gerald was born with legs so crooked they looked like parentheses. The doctor said he had to wait until Gerald was old enough to walk before he could fit him for braces, but after that his legs would be straight by the time he was two. But Gerald was almost four, and the only thing that had changed was that his leg braces were bigger. Roland was only one, and he was already practically walking better than Gerald.

"I took them off so he could use the toilet, what do you think?" Enid said. "Put them back on for me."

"What are we eating?" I asked as I stepped over Delta and Gerald and into the kitchen.

"Katu!" yelled Enid so loudly that both Delta and Gerald sucked in their breath and sat up abruptly.

"I forget sometimes," I said. "I'm sorry."

Haitian people believe that stepping over someone is as bad as sweeping their feet, only with different consequences. Sweeping their feet dooms them to a life without a husband or wife. Stepping over someone stunts that person's growth. Ma tells everyone Delta stopped growing after she got sick with pneumonia, but I think I probably stepped over her a hundred times when I was too young to appreciate what the tragic outcome would be.

I walked back to where Delta and Gerald sat on the floor, turned my back to them, and then took a giant backward step over them.

"Okay?" I asked Enid.

"I'm going to tell if you do that again."

"I won't do it again. I promise."

And I meant it. The first and only time the Daddy had caught me stepping over Gerald, he punched me in the head after instructing me to unstep him. That was the very first time I ever passed out.

I walked around Delta and Gerald in an exaggeratedly large semicircle. Enid rolled her eyes and shook her head.

"What's for dinner?" I asked again.

I admit I asked just to be annoying. I knew what we'd be eating: chicken and rice and beans and plantains. Or maybe beef and rice and beans and plantains. Or if Ma had had time to go to the Oriental market on Main Street and had time to remove all the bones, we might have fish and rice and beans and plantains. The plantains might be the sweet kind with the black and yellow skin or the hard kind with the black and green skin. And the beans might be red or they might be black or they might be green. But that's what we ate for dinner every day. Sometimes on a Saturday if we had been really, really good all day and no one had had to get a beat-up, then maybe we might get pizza or McDonald's or something. But that didn't happen an awful lot.

"Don't ask me that question, Katu," Enid answered. "You'll eat whatever I put on the table."

My mom cooked everything before she left for work, but Enid liked to act as if she'd made it. Enid stomped her foot in Delta's direction as she stood stirring the pot of rice and beans.

"Dee Dee, the table!" she yelled.

Our twin cousins, Jack and Joseph, came home as Delta set out seven plates, seven cups, five forks, and two spoons on the table. Jack and Joseph and their mom, my aunt Merlude, lived with us because they had just come from Haiti and couldn't make it on their own yet.

Jack and Joseph were nine and were supposed to be in the third grade, but because they didn't speak English, they attended Lincoln Elementary, which had an English-as-a-second-language class just for brand-new Haitian kids. They had different classes for the brand-new Vietnamese kids, the Russian kids, and the Chinese kids. As soon as Jack and Joseph learned enough English, they would be transferred to the same elementary school Delta and I had gone to. They were already learning real fast.

Jack zipped down the hallway and into the bedroom he shared with his mother and brother, and screamed. Enid and I got to the room and found Roland butt naked, shaking the poop from his diaper onto the floor.

"I told you to change his diaper, Katu!" yelled Enid. "You're cleaning this up."

"Why me?" I asked. "If you changed his diaper once in a while, instead of always waiting until I got home . . ."

Enid picked up the dirty diaper and threw it at my feet. Roland let out a shrieking laugh and ran out of the room. Enid followed him. I took the diaper and rolled it into a ball and headed into the kitchen to get wet paper towels.

"How you say 'poo-poo'?" Jack asked as he followed me down the hall.

I started to tell him to shut up but then turned and whispered, "Shit."

"Sheet?" he whispered back.

"Very good," I replied, and patted him on the shoulder.

By the time the poop had been cleaned off the floor and off Roland's butt, and Gerald's braces had been snapped onto his legs and we had all changed from our good school clothes into our house clothes, our dinner was cold.

"I'm not heating the food up," Enid announced as she hovered over the table with the pot of chicken.

"Why not?" asked Delta.

"If you all did what you were supposed to do when you were supposed to do it, we could have eaten before the food got cold," Enid replied, and grabbed the pot of plantains off the stove.

"Cold plantains are too hard to eat," I said. It was the green and black kind we were having that day. Sweet plantains don't harden as they cool.

"Tough," said Enid.

"And you're supposed to peel them before you serve them," I said.

I held up the half plantain that was my portion and squeezed it until clear slime seeped from underneath the rubbery peel. Plantains, whether sweet or not, are supposed to be peeled open and deslimed and deveined when it's easiest—while they're steaming hot.

Enid slammed the pot onto the stove, then disappeared down the hallway. We heard her stomping up the stairs. When she returned with the Daddy's belt, we were all intently peeling cold plantains with our fingers and cleaning off the slime with our nails. No one looked up as she draped the belt onto the back of her chair.

"Gerald and Ti Wo Wo don't have to eat cold food," said Enid to no one in particular. "They're just babies." Ma always set food for Gerald and Roland in a separate pot. It was the same food the rest of us ate, only she mushed it down until it was soft enough to swallow without much chewing.

Enid heated their portions, then sat with Roland on her lap to feed him. Gerald was old enough to feed himself, though most of his food ended up on his chair or on his clothing or stuck in the crevices of his leg braces.

Our dinner ritual was the same that afternoon as it was every weekday afternoon. The point of it all was to eat as much as we could without getting sick, then hide the rest before any adult came home. Ma and the Daddy's number one rule on food was that we had to eat every bit of what she cooked. The thing is Ma cooked enough for twelve kids, and there were only seven of us around. If she came home and discovered leftovers on a plate neatly wrapped in aluminum foil and tucked in the back of the refrigerator, she'd take it out and place it in the center of the table. Then she'd wake us up, march us all into the kitchen, and hand each of us a fork.

As we picked at the cold leftovers, Ma would wipe down the stove we'd already scrubbed, pull down dishes and cups we'd washed to check for spots, and sweep underneath the counters and behind the trash can, all the while reminding us that she and her brothers and sisters had never had any dinner when they were growing up in Haiti. Breakfast, neither. They might be lucky now and again to beg a pinkie-size chunk of rotten meat off a more fortunate neighbor to supplement the fistful of overcooked rice their parents could afford to provide for lunch. But when their stomachs growled at the setting sun, they couldn't just walk into an overflowing kitchen pantry and tear open a box of strawberry Fruit Roll-Ups or a bag of barbecue-flavored potato chips. Instead they fought one another over the last patch of beet red dirt around their shack that hadn't been marked by the village's stray dogs.

My mom sure can pile it on thick. I waited for the longest time for her to say that it was actually the village's stray dogs that hungry people fought over, but thank God she never went that far.

If we were still eating when Ma had finished recleaning the kitchen, she'd go into the hall closet and bring back the black-and-white photograph taken of her the day before she took two-year-old Enid and boarded an airplane out of Haiti.

"Look," she'd say as she tapped her middle finger against the glass. *"Eighty-nine pounds."*

In the photograph my mother is wearing a tank top, knee-length pants, and a pair of flip-flops. She is leaning against a brick wall, one hand on her hip. Her head is cocked, the way she always cocks it just before letting out a rare high-pitched, gap-toothed laugh. Her lips are pursed, and she is skinnier than I'm sure I'll ever see her again. She looks like a model.

Ma didn't know that those nighttime feedings weren't the only times we saw that photograph. Since starting high school, Enid had been taking the picture down to look at it before eating dinner. She used it as her diet inspiration, she explained. When we kids were alone at home, she refused to eat anything but a few bites of rice. And she said she ate only the fruit off her free lunch tray at school. Enid always made sure that the rest of us ate as much as we could, though. "You can go on a diet when you're old enough to have a boyfriend," she told me. I'd asked Enid if she had a boyfriend and if that's why she was always on a diet, but she would never answer. It's obvious now that she did have a boyfriend, but it wasn't until the night I got rid of the Daddy that I knew for sure. Like just about everything else, though, Delta knew long before I did.

When we were all too full to eat any more, Enid would offer rewards to the first person who could eat x number of bites in y minutes. Full mouthfuls only; she would judge who had cheated. The first prize was always the same: The winner would control what we watched on television that night. I'd sit out that round, having realized early on in the game that Enid always managed to talk the winner into picking her favorite television shows. Enid and I liked the same shows, especially *The A-Team* and *The Incredible Hulk*, so I saved what little room there was left in my stomach to win prize number two.

Prize number two was always better because Enid often made it up on the spot before she realized how much her promise would put her out in terms of time and patience. That afternoon Enid offered to do the after-dinner chore of whatever person ate three more bites in one minute. Then she translated into Creole for Jack and Joseph's benefit.

Jack and Joseph were never assigned house chores

when the adults were around because they were boys. Ma said girls had to learn how to keep a clean house as practice for when they got married. A Haitian boy, on the other hand, needed only the good sense to pick a great housecleaner to be his wife. As Delta, Enid, and I scrubbed the kitchen clean after each meal when Ma was home, Ma sent the boys outside to play, or into her room to watch television if the weather was bad.

The twins had taken their status as non-cleaning people for granted and had acted insulted when Enid first assigned them chores. Enid explained to them that when she was in charge of the house, everyone played by New York rules. Enid called them American rules when our boy cousins from Brooklyn and Chicago were visiting, but Jack and Joseph knew the strange white country they had landed in only as New York. The first rule was that when Enid was in charge of the house, everyone was a girl when it came to chores. Jack and Joseph had laughed at this and were immediately introduced to rule number two—the Daddy's belt. Enid had gleefully applied rule number two to Jack's and Joseph's behinds until they accepted rule number one.

Enid pointed at the wall clock, and the rest of us stared, with our forks in the air, waiting for the second hand to hit twelve.

"Wait a minute!" Delta yelled suddenly as the second hand passed eleven. "You didn't tell us what our chores are yet."

"Why does it matter, Dee Dee?" Enid asked. "If you win, I'm going to be doing it, not you."

I quickly realized Delta's point. "Yeah, but if my chore today is wiping the table, I'm not gonna stuff my face just to get out of that," I said.

"Tell us what our chores are first," said Delta. "Like, who has to wash the dishes?"

Enid grew agitated. "If I say who has to wash dishes and who has to scrub the stove, then only those two people will try to win the prize."

"But if you don't tell us, then none of us will try," I said. "And you'll be stuck with all this food."

Joseph pointed to his plantain and said, "Food." Jack pointed to his fork and said, "'Poon." They giggled.

"And if we do all try, you'll just say the winner's chore is to wipe the table, 'cause that's the easiest," said Delta.

Enid sighed and slid Roland off her lap and onto the floor. "Forget it," she said.

"No!" Delta and I yelled.

"No!" mimicked Jack and Joseph.

"Just tell us, Fee Fee," I whined.

"Oh, wait! I have an idea," Delta said. And it was a darn good one too. "Write down all the chores on little pieces of paper, then fold the papers and put them in a hat. After the contest the winner picks a piece of paper out of the hat, and you have to do that chore."

"Yeah!" I said. Then, "But we don't have a hat."

"We can use a pot," Delta said.

"Yeah!"

Enid looked at the clock. "Daddy will be here soon," she said. It was four fifteen. The Daddy came home for dinner every day at four thirty.

"We'll hurry," I said as I pulled a notebook out of my backpack. Delta pulled a small saucepan out of the cabinet. Enid tore a sheet of notebook paper into several smaller pieces, quickly scribbled on each, then tossed the balled-up papers into the pan.

"When the second hand is on the twelve, start eating," said Enid. "Okay . . . go!"

Joseph took a sip of his milk, then picked up his plantain with his bare hands and shoved it into his mouth. He used his fingers to pinch his lips together to keep the mixture from falling out. He chewed a few times, but when he saw Jack and me take our third bites, he opened his mouth and let saliva and milk-softened plantain chunks fall back onto his plate. He took a gasp of air and announced, *"Fini."*

Enid was distracted by Joseph and didn't notice that the second hand was quickly making its return to the twelve and that Jack and I were in a chew-for-chew dead heat. I slapped the table to get her attention.

"Go, go, go!" she yelled, swinging her head from me to Jack and back again. "Chew faster!"

I decided to forgo chewing altogether. I drank from my glass of milk, swallowed the rest of my food as if it were a pill, then stuck out my tongue.

"And the winner iiiis . . ." Enid grabbed my arm and lifted it up into the air. "Ka-*rrr*-ina!"

Jack spit the rest of his food out onto his plate.

"You guys are so disgusting," said Delta. Jack and Joseph smiled blankly at her.

"Okay, now just pick one," said Enid as she held the pan just over my head.

"Bring it down," I said.

"Pick one!" she said, and stomped her foot.

I reached above my head and into the pan. I grabbed the first ball of paper I touched. Inside, written in Enid's awful handwriting, was "Wipe the table." Enid grabbed it from me. I groaned.

"Let's get rid of this stuff," said Enid.

We separated the leftover food onto two plates. Chicken and plantains on one plate; rice, beans, and Gerald and Roland's leftover mush on another. Jack and Delta took the mush plate into the hallway bathroom.

Joseph slipped a long yellow dishwashing glove over each hand, then dug into the kitchen garbage, pushing aside dirty diapers, cigarette butts, eggshells, and the rest of that day's trash, until he reached the middle. As Enid used a fork to push the chicken and plantains off the plate and into the hole Joseph had created, I heard a car door slam.

"He's here!" I yelled.

Enid snapped the lid back onto the garbage can and dragged it into the corner. Delta and Jack came running out of the bathroom. Jack dropped the empty plate into the sink and took a seat at the table next to Joseph. Delta began frantically clearing the table, and Enid started washing the pots and pans. I grabbed a broom and kept my eye on the front door. I started sweeping underneath the table, carefully avoiding Jack's and Joseph's dangling feet.

"Where are you?" yelled the Daddy.

"In the kitchen!" Enid replied.

The Daddy walked in and headed straight for the stove. He opened the oven door and pulled out a large covered pot from the top rack. He handed it to Enid and said, "Heat this."

The Daddy walked over to the head of the table, the side farthest from the sink and stove, and dropped all three hundred pounds of himself into the chair. The cushion let out a loud fart.

"Ti Wo Wo!" the Daddy yelled. Roland, who had stopped in his crawling tracks when the Daddy entered the kitchen, giggled, struggled to his feet, and toddled halfway to his father before falling onto his butt again.

"Daddy," he said.

I set the broom against the wall and picked Roland up. He stretched his arms toward his father. "Daddy," he repeated. I kissed the Daddy on the cheek, then placed Roland into his lap.

"Hi, Daddy," I whispered.

Delta came over and kissed the Daddy hello. Then Enid. Jack and Joseph got up from their seats, came around the table, and stood in front of their uncle. *"Bon jou, mononcle,"* they said almost in unison before returning to their seats. With the heavy braces on his legs, Gerald couldn't move without help. He sat in the same position he'd been in since we first sat down to dinner.

The Daddy reached over to him and slapped the metal on his legs. "You still hungry?" the Daddy asked in Creole. Gerald shook his head vigorously.

"Yes you are," said the Daddy.

Gerald giggled. "No I'm not," he replied in English.

"You must still be hungry," the Daddy said. "Why else are you sitting at the table?"

Gerald giggled again, then fingered one of the metal bars connecting his left leg brace to his right.

Enid placed the Daddy's dinner in front of him and handed him a fork and a paper towel. She returned to the stove and piled another plate with food. That was for the Daddy too.

I think if dogs ate with a fork, they'd probably look a lot like the Daddy doing it. He kept his face so close to the plate he could have just stretched his lips out and yanked them back with a mouthful of rice. He never looked up from his plate until he was finished. Ma said that the Daddy ate that way because eating isn't a game. She said we should all eat like that.

The Daddy finally sat back in his chair, breathing heavily and picking his teeth with his pinkie fingernail. He sighed, then said, "Okay."

"Are you going back to work?" asked Gerald.

"You have money?" asked the Daddy.

Gerald shook his head. The Daddy heaved himself out of the chair and walked into the hallway.

"Who left the bathroom light on?" the Daddy asked.

Delta sucked in her breath and slapped her mouth.

"You flushed the toilet, right?" I whispered.

Delta's eyes zigzagged around the kitchen, then settled on Jack. Jack shrugged.

"I no remember," he whispered.

When the Daddy came back into the kitchen, he was walking real slowly and jangling change in his pant pocket. He was still picking at his teeth with his other hand. He looked around the room, stopping his gaze on us one at a time. We all stared back.

"Did you finish all your food today, Gerald?" He didn't take his finger out of his mouth to ask. Gerald looked to Enid for help, then looked back at his father. He hesitated another moment, then nodded.

"Gerald finish all his food today?" He was looking at Enid now.

Enid said, "Ummm . . . ," and twisted her eyebrows into her best *Now, let me see if I remember correctly* look. She had only gotten out half a nod, her neck stretching up, her jaw sticking out just slightly, when the Daddy's teeth-picking hand flew out of his mouth with all the fingers curled in and caught her on the cheek.

Enid flew back toward the stove. The oven door handle karate-chopped her just above her butt, and she broke backward onto the stovetop. Enid didn't yell. The only sound came from her knees and then elbows hitting the floor as she fell.

3.

You'd think that as many times as we'd gotten beat-ups from the Daddy, we'd all have learned how to duck or maybe throw our arms up in front of our face. But the Daddy had so many beat-up moods and so many beat-up techniques, it was hard to see which was coming and when. It was sometimes even hard to predict who would be getting a beat-up, even when it was obvious to all that there was a beat-up to be had.

That afternoon Enid would be getting it. That was made clear in the second it took for Gerald to look her way when the Daddy asked about his dinner.

The moment before a beat-up is kinda like the moment before going into a haunted house. You know before you even go in that you're going to be scared. You just don't know exactly when the monster is going to jump out of the corner and yell, "Boo!" And even though you're prepared, it's a surprise every time, and you end up screaming and knocking your kid sister to the floor to get to someplace safe. Except with a haunted house you can always leave and never go back.

So when the monster yelled "Boo" that afternoon, Jack, Joseph, Delta, and I ran into the bathroom. At least, we did eventually. First we tripped and fell over one another, trying to get out of the kitchen. Then we tripped and fell over one another in the hallway. Then we shoved, fell, and stepped all over one another into the bathroom. I slammed the door closed with my entire body, and the rest of them fell against me. The way we were gasping for breath, you'd have thought we'd just run a marathon instead of the dozen steps from the kitchen to the bathroom.

I know what you're thinking. We left the babies in the kitchen. But that always happened. No matter how many times I told myself to grab Gerald and told Delta to grab Roland, they always got left behind and we had to go back and get them. I didn't feel too bad, though, because when I was the one getting the beat-up, Enid sometimes ran off without the babies too.

I looked at Delta and said nothing, but she nodded. I opened the door, and we tiptoed out into the hallway. Gerald and Roland were wailing full blast by now, so loud I couldn't tell if Enid had started yet.

We came into the kitchen just as one of the Daddy's kicks landed on Enid's thigh. She was still on the floor. Roland was so close to her Enid could have reached out and touched him if her arms weren't busy jumping from her head to her stomach, then her legs. It wasn't much help; the Daddy's foot always made it to whatever part you were trying to protect before your arms did.

Delta danced from one foot to the other, shaking and crying, before she got the courage to snatch Roland by one arm and drag him across the kitchen floor and out to the hallway. Gerald was sitting in his chair with his arms stretched out to me. He was too heavy for me to carry when his leg braces were on, but there was no way I was going to stay in that kitchen and take the time to take them off. I grabbed him underneath the arms and yanked him off the chair. His metal legs made a scraping sound as they hit the floor. I started backing out of the kitchen, pulling him in front of me.

Then the Daddy stopped kicking Enid.

"Stand up," he said.

Enid's cries sound like when a person upchucks. Only, instead of food it's spit and snot and tears that come out of her. So every time she heaved in, her body curled out of the fetal position just a little, then went back tight, chin to knees, as she heaved out, half upchucking, half howling.

"Stand up," the Daddy repeated. Enid stayed squirming around on the floor. The Daddy turned toward the table and came straight toward me. I froze. He walked around Gerald and me to the chair where Enid had hung his belt. He folded the belt in two—tip to buckle—as he watched Enid heaving in and heaving out. There was a look on his face like he was tired or annoyed. Like he had better things to do than beat his stepdaughter but he had no choice; it was his responsibility. It was the way Ma looks when we're standing in line at the supermarket and the Hasidic family in front of us has three grocery carts filled with food and even more kids bouncing around than she does. Head cocked, fist to hip, when it comes to dealing with kids—feeding them or beating them—apparently there is always something better to be doing. The Daddy bit his lower lip and tightened his grip around the belt loop.

"Why don't you find your own father and squeeze money out of his head," said the Daddy. "Then you can do whatever you want with the food he buys. Stand up."

Heave in. Heave out.

"Who dumped the food into the toilet?" the Daddy asked. But he wasn't asking Enid. He was looking at me. Gerald and I were standing between him and Enid. My arms were beginning to hurt from holding Gerald up. I started to hyperventilate.

"Stand up, Enid," I said after what seemed like an eternity to calm my breathing down. *"Pleeeease."*

There was no reason for both of us to get a beat-up at this point. It wasn't the same thing when the beat-ups hadn't begun yet, when Delta and I would sometimes tell on each other to escape the belt or the electrical cord or some appliance or other that the Daddy decided to test out that day. When he'd already picked someone and the beat-up had begun, there was no need to spread it around. Someone else's turn would come around the next day or the day after that.

I know it was a mean thing to do to Enid, though, because she'd never once ratted out me or Delta to get out of a beat-up, even when she'd had every right to do it.

"You're not going to get up?" the Daddy asked Enid.

Enid uncurled herself and started to get to her

knees. I grabbed my wrists at Gerald's chest and backed out of the kitchen. When I got to the bathroom door, I heard the belt make a *whishhh* sound through the air and then land on flesh. Enid screamed. Not her upchuck-sounding scream, but a real girl-who's-seen-a-mouse earsplitter. Delta let me into the bathroom. I dragged Gerald in and dropped him near the tub as Delta locked the door behind us.

"Next time you flush the toilet," I said to Delta. She nodded and reached for the handle. I slapped her hand away.

"Not now," I said. "He already saw it. We might get in more trouble. Let's wait until he leaves."

Gerald and Roland had not stopped crying, and locked in the bathroom with them, it was hard to make out what was going on in the kitchen. All I could hear were thumps. Some might have been Enid slamming against the wall or stove, some might have been the Daddy doing that barking grunt he does when he gets really carried away. I couldn't hear Enid screaming anymore, but after a while of being beaten, she starts to choke on her screams anyway. We all do.

I don't know how long we were in the bathroom, but it seemed liked so much longer than usual. I had taken off Gerald's leg braces, and he was sitting in my lap, still crying but not so loud. Jack and Joseph sat shoulder to shoulder up against the washing machine. Roland fell asleep with his thumb in his mouth on the bath mat wrapped around the toilet. Delta picked up Roland and put him back down on the mat in front of the sink. Then she knelt in front of the toilet, tugged at her necklace until her gold cross came out of her shirt, put her elbows on the lid, and clapped her hands in front of her face. The gold cross dangled at her chin.

As long as Delta didn't get too carried away with her praying, I didn't mind it. Sometimes, though, she'd act like she was bitten by the Holy Ghost, yelling to Jesus to forgive our sins and for angels to come save us. Aunt Merlude is Pentecostal, and so the twins are used to crazy church people. But we are Catholic, and Delta's carrying on like that only upset our little brothers even more. When it was me getting a beat-up, Enid wouldn't let Delta pray at all. That afternoon Delta settled for whispering the Lord's Prayer over and over again.

"'Our Father, who art in heaven, hallowed be Thy name, Thy kingdom come, Thy will be done, on earth as it is in heaven.'"

Gerald eventually stopped crying—the Lord's Prayer had put him in a trance—and when he fell asleep, we could hear the Daddy grunting and yelling at Enid to stand up even after Enid had stopped making any noises that we could hear. Then after, like, a million years the Daddy stopped yelling, but we could hear him moving around the kitchen.

Delta made the sign of the cross, then looked up from the toilet and asked, "You think he's getting ready to go back to work?"

"Yeah," I said.

The Daddy made his best money in the evening. He drove a taxi around the county. Around six or seven is when a lot of white people come home from working in the city, and the Haitian women who are their baby-sitters and house cleaners need rides to their own homes. The Jamaican ladies and the Puerto Ricans need rides too. But the Jamaicans have their own taxis, and the Puerto Ricans are mostly all the way on the other side of the county.

The Daddy liked to say he owned his own taxi company because he had two cars with his name painted on them. His brother Jude drove the other one, but just barely. Most of the time Uncle Jude was too drunk to get out of his apartment. And when he did get out to work, he'd usually pick up one woman at a time, not the five or six the Daddy would jam into his car. The Daddy's taxi was one of those big red round ones. You know, with the two extra little backward-facing seats in back? Anyway, I heard the two of them fighting one time. The Daddy said that Uncle Jude was going to put him out of business right before some woman's husband got the two of them mixed up and shot the Daddy dead. Uncle Jude said that the Daddy should run his company like a professional—like they did in the city. You didn't see white people putting up with sharing rides with a hundred other passengers, did you? That's what Uncle Jude asked.

I heard the Daddy tell Ma that he wouldn't have to work so much if Uncle Jude worked half as hard as the Daddy did. Aunt Merlude asked why he didn't just fire Uncle Jude and get someone else to drive the taxi. There were so many Haitian men wanting to get their families out of the city to a nice place in upstate New York like Chestnut Valley, where their kids could grow up with white people's kids and not end up sounding like the blacks, Aunt Merlude said. But the Daddy didn't answer. Later Ma told Aunt Merlude that no one else would work for the Daddy. They were too afraid. Only a few years out of Haiti and already he had the same reputation all over the country of New York that he'd had back home. To tell the truth, I was glad Uncle Jude stayed drunk so much that the Daddy had to work all the time. Otherwise he'd have been home more.

Anyway, like I was saying, we were in that bathroom forever that afternoon. After the Daddy stomped around awhile, it got real quiet. We figured he'd left the house through the sliding glass doors in the kitchen and that's why we didn't hear him come past the bathroom. So I snuck into the hallway. When I turned the corner to the kitchen, I saw him standing half in and half out the back door, smoking a cigarette.

The Daddy had gone really nuts this time. It looked like a tornado had hit the kitchen. And Enid—I didn't know if she was dead or what. She was bunched up against the stove, not moving a muscle. Her back was to me, so I couldn't see if her chest was moving up and down. I think I was wishing her to breathe so hard that the Daddy heard me breathing and turned and looked at me. I almost fainted, I swear.

But he didn't do anything. And he didn't say a word. Only jangled the change in his pocket and smoked.

Then he looked over at Enid real quick and stepped outside and slid the door shut. I didn't move until I heard his taxi back out of the driveway.

When I turned Enid onto her back, she looked like she was dead. Her mouth was open, and there was drool and blood on her face and all down her neck. Her eyes were swollen, but they looked like they might be open under all the puffiness. Some of the buttons on her shirt had popped off, and I could see blood on her stomach, seeping out from patches of skin that looked like they had been burned. There was blood coming through her pants, too. I didn't know if it was the same blood from her stomach or if her legs were also bleeding. I thought maybe she really was dead, but when I picked her arm up and let it drop, it fell right to the floor. Dead people are supposed to be stiff.

"Enid!" I yelled with my mouth right in her ear. "Wake up!" She didn't budge.

"You have to throw cold water on her." I looked up and saw Delta and Jack and Joseph standing in the hallway. "The cold will bring her back to consciousness," said Delta as she walked over to the kitchen sink.

Delta filled a cup with water and handed it to me. I began pouring it over Enid's head.

"Not like you're baptizing her," said Delta as she took the cup from me and filled it up again. "Like this," she said, and took two giant steps back from Enid before throwing the water at her.

Enid coughed once and swung her head from one

side to the other and stopped. The water that had gotten into her nose was running out, mixed with snot and blood, sideways down her cheek.

"Get up, Enid!" I yelled again, and this time I started shaking her shoulders. Delta began pulling on her arm. While Delta and I were crouched over Enid, Jack filled the cup with more water. He threw it at Enid, soaking me and Delta, too. But this time Enid sat up fast, like she had just woken up from a nightmare.

"Fee Fee!" Delta and I yelled together.

Enid had this look in her eyes—well, in her one decent eye that wasn't too swollen—she had this look like she was alone in the kitchen, like she didn't see any of us and didn't know we were there. It was only a split second, and just as fast as she had sat up, she fell back down. She let out a loud sigh. Then her eye rolled funny and closed.

4.

"She's dead, she's dead!" Delta wailed. "Please, God, help us! She's dead!" Delta collapsed next to Enid and began screaming.

Jack and Joseph practically jumped on Enid and started yelling for her to get up. *"Lève! Lève!"*

I heard the babies crying in the bathroom, and all of a sudden I had to pee really bad.

Gerald was crawling toward the door when I got to the bathroom. I stepped over him and pulled down my pants. I didn't care then whether or not he stopped growing, not while Enid was lying on the kitchen floor, near death. I'd never been so nervous in my life. People who are nervous on television say they have butterflies in their stomach. There may have been butterflies coming out of me that day; there may have been monkeys and elephants, too. I was sure once every last scrap of food I'd ever eaten had come out, next would come my intestines, then my stomach, and eventually my brain would ooze out, and they'd find me, bone and shriveled skin, draped across the toilet.

Right then I wished that was exactly what would happen—that I would die right there in the bathroom, because with Enid hurt so bad, it meant that I was in charge, and I had no idea what to do. My legs were bouncing so hard and fast I had to reach down and shove Roland off the toilet mat to avoid crushing him under my sneakers.

I looked up at the pink and white butterfly clock hanging near the medicine cabinet: 6:16. Aunt Merlude would be home at 6:38. Sometimes when it was raining hard or the snow was real deep, the Daddy would pick Aunt Merlude up from the Mrs.'s house, and she'd make it home before six. Otherwise Aunt Merlude left the Mrs.'s house at 5:35 and caught the 5:57 number 11 bus seven blocks away. Then she'd ride to the corner of Main and Fairview and walk the four blocks home from there. I had to go with Aunt Merlude the first two times to show her the way. I could catch the 5:48 13R and make it home by 6:15 if I had to do it by myself. But every month Aunt Merlude gained a few more pounds and added a couple more minutes to her commute home.

I didn't die that afternoon, obviously. Jack came knocking on the door. Or maybe it was Joseph. "Come, Katu," cried whichever twin it was. And as soon as I heard that whimper, I remembered something.

Several months earlier, on the first Sunday after Aunt Merlude and Jack and Joseph moved in with us, all our Brooklyn relatives showed up at the house. My cousins and their moms and dads, Ma's cousins and some of their kids, my grandmother, other old women who insisted, "You remember me, don't you?" and squeezed my cheek so hard I bit the inside of my mouth and had blood oozing through my teeth.

Anyway, at that point Joseph and Jack were still getting used to the idea that a bed was something with metal legs and a top that could double as a bouncing play area, and not a couple of blankets laid out on a floor and folded away in the morning. Who knows if they would have stopped jumping up and down on their new bed if Aunt Mary Jean's baby hadn't howled once after rolling off the bed and hitting the floor headfirst before passing out. I got to the bedroom right behind my aunt.

"Bon Dieu!" she yelled, and managed to smack both Jack and Joseph off the bed with one swing of her arm. Then she called her husband while yanking the top sheet off the bed. Aunt Mary Jean had the sheet folded a few times by the time her husband got there. He knew just what she was doing.

He grabbed an end of the sheet with one hand and with the other hand grabbed the baby and put him in the center of the shortened sheet. He then raised his arms so that the baby rolled from his side of the sheet to Aunt Mary Jean's, then he lowered his arms and Aunt Mary Jean raised her arms. Pretty soon the baby was bouncing between them like the ball in a game of keep-away. Right when I thought for sure the baby was going to miss the sheet and come crashing to the floor, my aunt and uncle slowed down, then stopped. Weird, yeah. But it worked. The baby started crying.

When I got to the kitchen with the sheet from my

bed, Enid was where I had left her. Delta was crying quietly with her head on Enid's shoulder.

"Remember when Aunt Mary Jean's baby fell off the bed?" I asked. Delta looked up at me.

"She's too heavy," Delta whined.

"We have to try," I said. I folded the sheet in two and laid it out next to Enid. Delta helped me roll her onto the sheet. We didn't need to say anything to Jack and Joseph. They understood. Joseph stood next to me, and Jack moved over to Delta's side and picked up a corner of the sheet.

"Okay, Jack and Dee Dee . . . lift," I said. Delta was right. Enid was heavier than I thought. They managed to lift her head and her legs, but her butt stayed on the floor.

"Higher," I said. Delta and Jack walked the sheet toward Joseph and me. Enid's body rolled once, and she landed stomach down. Her chest rested on my hands, her legs on Joseph's hands.

"Now you guys walk back," I said as I jutted my chin to Delta and Jack. "Joseph, lift."

Joseph and I lifted our side of the sheet and walked forward while Delta and Jack walked back. Enid rolled once again and she was on her back.

"Okay . . . again." Delta was sweating already. Jack and Joseph grunted with each step forward and inhaled with each step back. My heart was pounding. I didn't think we were getting Enid any closer to waking up, but I didn't know what else to do. I was afraid if I let us give up, I'd be on the floor with Delta shrieking and crying.

"Higher," I repeated as Delta and Jack walked forward, and "Lift," I chanted as Joseph and I rolled the sheet. Suddenly, on my fourth or fifth "Lift," Jack took one step back and dropped his corner of the sheet. Enid's head thudded to the kitchen floor. Jack took off running toward his mother.

"What you doing?" asked Aunt Merlude as she entered the kitchen.

"What you doing?" was Aunt Merlude's favorite phrase. Besides "No 'peak de English" and "All clean for you, Mrs. I come tomorrow," it was about all the English she knew at that point. She looked around at the mess in the kitchen and then down at Enid. By the smile still on her face I figured she thought we were playing a game. Then her eyes focused on the blood near the stove. Just about then Jack unburied his head from her side to let out the wail he'd been working on.

"Fee Fee *mouri!*" he screamed. It took a moment more for Aunt Merlude to register it all. Remember I told you that Aunt Merlude is Pentecostal? You know how they are, don't you? Aunt Merlude took one step closer to Enid, and I thought we were going to have church right there over her body. She raised her hands over her head and shook them. Her mouth was opened wide, but nothing came out. Then she grabbed her boobs and, bouncing up and down from one leg to the other, yelled in Creole, "Jesus! Jesus! Jesus, Mary, Joseph!"

We all started crying again. Joseph dropped to the floor and began shaking Enid, crying, "Fee Fee! Fee Fee!" All the time, though, he kept his eyes on his mother. I think Joseph wanted Enid to wake up and be okay just so that his mother could stop the fits that were getting wilder and scarier by the second.

Aunt Merlude stopped calling on Jesus and his family just long enough to ask us what we had done to poor Enid. She didn't hear Delta say it was the Daddy. Delta then began pacing around the kitchen, chanting, "Nine-one-one, nine-one-one. Call nine-one-one." She was swinging her head back and forth, as if looking for the telephone.

We had no telephone in the kitchen, and I was suddenly glad about that. The last beat-up that was so bad we thought of 911 had been when Delta tripped over her hula hoop while carrying Roland to his crib and dropped him on the floor. Roland cried some, but he wasn't hurt. When the Daddy was done with Delta, though, she couldn't stand up. Her eyes rolled funny like Enid's had just done, and after she closed them, she wet her pants. Ma walked in as I was dialing 911 and grabbed the phone from me.

"Who is going to pay for the house when they put him in jail?" she had asked. "You? And you will pay the electric and the water and buy food to put on the table?"

I don't know how long I lost track of Delta. I'd been staring at Aunt Merlude, and I must have fallen into a trance. She was speaking in tongues now, down on the floor with Enid, rocking her back and forth. So much for hoping a grown-up would show up and take over.

I found Delta in the hallway with the telephone in

her hand, staring at it like she couldn't remember the number for 911. I grabbed it from her and hung it up.

"He'll get arrested if we call the police," I said. "Then who is going to pay the bills around here? You?"

Delta choked in several gulps of air, then quietly let it all out. She dropped her shoulders and rubbed her eyes. I knew what she'd do next. Delta's reaction to really bad chaos is always the same—calm, prayer, hysteria, sleep. I was already surprised at how long her calm period had lasted that day. But the hysteria and sleep parts arrived as I expected. And the problem is the sleep period usually ends with Delta wetting the bed.

I'd say out of the million and one things that could send the Daddy off into a rage, peeing in the bed was right up there with throwing out food. The Daddy wanted to punish Delta the way he said kids in Haiti got punished for wetting the bed. He wanted to drape the wet sheet around her shoulders, march her out to the corner of our block in her pajamas, and have her tell everyone passing by that she was a bed wetter. Ma quickly shot down that idea by reminding the Daddy that the only people Americans despised more than those who hurt children were those who hurt dogs, and so he might end up in prison. The Daddy asked how standing on a street corner for a couple of hours could hurt anybody, but Ma just sucked her teeth and turned away.

The Daddy had to settle for just beat-ups as punishment for wetting the bed, but for a while Delta was really screwed anyway. She'd start out calmly handing Daddy the belt already folded over the way he liked it, then offering her arms to him. The first lick would send her into hysterics, then after the beat-up she'd wind down and fall asleep and then wet the bed and then get the Daddy the belt and do it all over again. Finally Enid and I decided that Delta should just sleep on the floor on any day someone got a beat-up. For a couple of years until the Daddy died, Delta almost never slept in the bed she and I shared.

As I turned from her and jumped down the four steps to the front door in one leap, I yelled, "Remember to sleep on the floor, Dee Dee!"

Uncle Jude lived in the Royal Gardens apartment complex about six blocks from our place. That's where I finally decided to go. I didn't bother calling first because Uncle Jude's phone was almost always disconnected. Why bother paying the phone bill, he said, when the only calls the phone company would let through were from other bill collectors?

I had been knocking on the door to apartment 3J for a couple of minutes before I heard Uncle Jude stumbling around the other side. He finally opened the door and stared down at me like I was a complete stranger. Then he looked behind me and up and down the hallway. Uncle Jude looked just like the Daddy. Only Uncle Jude was as amazingly tall and skinny as the Daddy was amazingly short and fat. When they stood in front of each other, it was like watching one man watch himself in a fun-house mirror.

"Where everybody is this fine, fine, eh, beautiful evening, my sweetheart?" he asked.

When Uncle Jude is drunk, he likes to show off his English, only he doesn't seem to understand any of it himself. And when I'm stressed out, my Creole is even more like gibberish than it normally is. So I reverted to the universal code for "Stop screwing around and come help me." I started sobbing loudly and at the same time backing away from the door and flapping my hands toward my body.

"Wait a little minute," said Uncle Jude as he disappeared behind the door. I heard keys jangling and slippers shuffling around. He was back in a flash. Uncle Jude fell only once going down the three flights of stairs to the parking lot. But that once was enough. I grabbed the car keys from him and jumped into the driver's side of his taxi. He looked around the parking lot to see if anyone was watching, but he didn't protest.

Don't look at me like that. Who would you rather have driving? The guy so drunk he can't remember which language he speaks, or the sober thirteen-year-old? Besides, Uncle Jude had already taught me how to drive by that point. Ma would sometimes send me with him for errands that the Daddy couldn't be bothered to do. After we did our shopping, Uncle Jude would drive over to the school district administration building. Their parking lot is huge and always empty on Saturdays. He'd let me practice driving up and down the parking rows and making U-turns while he relaxed with a beer or two or three. He'd been letting me drive since I was ten. It was our little secret. I even almost learned how to parallel park. Uncle Jude had me use the RESERVED FOR SUPERINTENDENT spot tucked between the building and an old elm tree. When I hit the building backing into the spot, Uncle Jude spilled half a can of beer onto his lap. He was pretty peeved.

"You know how much money this cost?" he asked.

I thought he was talking about the taxi, but when I looked over at him, he was staring at the beer pooling between his legs like he was calculating how much of it he could rescue if he bent down right then and started sucking the seat dry.

"You don't need parallel park, sweetheart," he sighed. "You have driveway."

"Okay, okay, my sweetheart," Uncle Jude repeated now as I told him of Enid's beat-up on the drive over to the house. I told him some in English and some in Creole and didn't really care if he didn't completely understand. He would when he saw Enid. Aunt Merlude was still on the kitchen floor with Enid when Uncle Jude and I made it back to the house. Only now she was whispering a prayer in Creole. Enid still looked awful, but she didn't look so dead anymore. She looked like she was just sleeping. Her mouth was closed and she wasn't drooling. Jack and Joseph were so quiet and cramped into a corner of the kitchen that I didn't notice them at first. They were holding on to each other and staring at their mother.

Aunt Merlude wrinkled her nose, then jerked her head back and opened her eyes. Uncle Jude was bent down over her and Enid. He rubbed Enid's arms and softly called her name. Then he keeled over, right onto the two of them.

"Oh, Jesus!" yelled Aunt Merlude.

"There must be some water here on the floor," said Uncle Jude. "It's slippery."

I ran over and grabbed two of his belt loops and began pulling. Suddenly I heard an awful cry, and Uncle Jude came flying backward, falling onto me.

"Fee Fee!" I heard Aunt Merlude yell.

Uncle Jude and I untangled ourselves but stayed on the floor and watched as Enid fought off imaginary attackers, kicking her legs wildly and punching at the air. Aunt Merlude did her best to hold her still. When Enid had calmed down some, Aunt Merlude said to me, "Go fill the tub with hot water."

Roland and Gerald were no longer in the bathroom. I found them asleep in my bedroom, curled up on the floor next to Delta. I picked up Roland and carried him to his crib in Ma's room. He stayed asleep as I changed his diaper. When I got back to the kitchen, Aunt Merlude and Uncle Jude had Enid up on her feet, but they were practically carrying her toward the hallway bathroom. Enid was moaning. I stepped to the side to let them out of the kitchen.

"Katu, bring the salt," said Aunt Merlude.

Aunt Merlude had Enid propped against the dryer and was removing her clothes. Uncle Jude took the salt from me and poured some into the tub. He used his hand to stir the water. Enid was covered in welts and dried blood. Aunt Merlude guided her into the tub, and Uncle Jude helped lower her in. When Enid's butt hit the water, she started screaming and tried to get up. Uncle Jude held her down as Aunt Merlude began scooping tub water with an empty coffee can and pouring it on Enid's top half.

When I couldn't take the screaming anymore, I went back into the kitchen. Jack and Joseph hadn't moved. They looked drained and exhausted. Jack stared at the ceiling. Joseph was picking peeling paint chips off the wall, flicking some into the air, sticking others into his mouth. I picked up the chairs that had been flung about and arranged them around the table, then got the mop and began cleaning the floor. I hadn't noticed the odor before, but now it was obvious. The goop on the floor wasn't just blood and snot and water. Enid had peed on herself too.

When I was done with the floor, I finished washing the dishes. The pot we had used in our eating game sat on the counter off to the side. One by one I pulled open all the little scraps of paper before tossing them into the trash. They all said the same thing: "Wipe the table."

"Let's go," I said to Jack and Joseph as I took the Daddy's belt off the table, rolled the soiled sheet into a ball, and left the kitchen. Uncle Jude came out of the bathroom just as we entered the hallway. We heard Enid crying and Aunt Merlude praying, but none of us even looked toward the door.

"Where mom's job number?" asked Uncle Jude. I pointed to the strip of notebook paper taped to the hallway table next to the telephone, then headed up the stairs. Jack and Joseph followed me instead of going into their own room. I checked on Roland in his crib, then opened the closet door and hung the Daddy's belt on the nail with his two church ties. I dropped the sheet into the hamper in Ma's bathroom. Jack and Joseph were in my bed when I got to my room. I crawled in with them and went to sleep, not bothering to change into my pajamas first.

5.

It was very early when I opened my eyes the morning after Enid's beat-up, still dark. There were people in the house who weren't normally there. It was something I sensed more than actually knew for sure. You know how you get used to people's footsteps when you live with them? Or the particular *hmmm-hmmmm-bzzz-hmm* sounds you hear that let you know just who is speaking even though you can't make out what they're saying? I heard all that. Ma was one of the people down there. The others I couldn't tell.

Then the faint sound of church music started. A group of nasally women slapping their hands together and praising Jesus a cappella. Something about the music was strange. It seemed to be coming from directly below our bedroom, from Aunt Merlude's room instead of from the stereo in the living room, at the other end of the house. The song ended with a high-pitched, drawn-out "Amen," and then I heard a sound—someone cleared their throat.

I freed my left arm from underneath Gerald. Sometime during the night he had hauled himself into the bed with me and the twins, leaving Delta alone on the floor, half in and half out of the closet, wrapped in a comforter. I wasn't surprised that Enid wasn't in the room. Her bed was empty.

When I opened the bedroom door, light from the rest of the house flooded in and blinded me for a second. It seemed as if someone had hit every switch they could find. From the top of the stairs I swore I could tell that even the stove light was on, burning that brown orange glow because of all the grease and flecks of food caked on it. I tiptoed down the stairs and into the hallway.

Surrounding the open door to Aunt Merlude's room were four really fat women singing, clapping, and swaying with their eyes closed. I didn't recognize all of them, but I knew they had to be from Aunt Merlude's church. Pentecostal women never wear pants or any jewelry other than a wedding ring. And whenever there is a crisis, before a priest or pastor is called, before a doctor or police officer arrives, the church women come. Their presence here was not a good sign. One had tears rolling down her face.

I stayed watching as their song came to an end, and then they all began praying out loud. They weren't all saying the same prayer like we do in Catholic church. They each said their own made-up-on-the-spot prayer. They all started quietly and got louder and louder, until our house sounded like the school auditorium at assembly time when all the grades have been seated but the principal hasn't yet said, "Boys and girls, may I have your attention, please."

I walked quickly past them to the edge of the

kitchen entrance and poked my head around the corner. It was worse than I thought. My aunt Jacqueline was there. She had come up from Brooklyn sometime during the night. Brooklyn was only a couple hours away from us, but it wasn't a trip Aunt Jacqueline or Ma arranged on the fly. There were preparations to be made. New outfits to be bought or to have Augustin make. The more lace and frills the better. Ma had three heads besides her own that had to be washed, hot-set, hot-pressed, curled, and combed. That alone took a half a day, so it was always done the night before. After all the yanking and pulling at our scalps, aspirin had become our regular night-before-visiting-day bedtime treat. Delta and Enid were real good at sleeping on their stomach with their chin propped on folded hands like perfectly coiffed angels. I was pretty much hit or miss. And when I missed, Ma would be there waiting for me bright and early in the morning, the heavy metal comb on the stove, the leftover hairs in its teeth sizzling and smoking in the fire.

Then there was the bathing. For some reason, as old as we were, Ma didn't trust us with our own personal hygiene on special occasions. I know I can trust you to keep that to yourself, right? Good. 'Cause what she'd do was call us into the bathroom one by one on visiting-day morning and scrub us from head to toe. Well, technically it was face to toe. And she wouldn't use a washcloth or her hands. Nope. A pumice stone. When it was all over and we were nice and raw, she'd pour baby oil on us, pat us dry, sprinkle us with baby powder, hand us a brand-new pair of panties, and send us to get dressed.

Whether we were the visitors or the visitees, the home team or the away team, our cousins always looked like we did—itchy, head achy, and anxious for the end of visiting day. The only saving grace was that visiting between Brooklyn and Chestnut Valley was done only because it was Easter weekend or because of an especially good event, like a baby being born or someone getting married or coming in from Haiti for the first time, or because of an especially bad event, like someone dying.

My mom was sitting at the kitchen table, and when the church ladies quieted down with the praying and started up on the singing again, I could hear that Ma was telling Aunt Jacqueline what had happened the day before.

". . . right here in the kitchen yelling for her life, yelling for her mother. And you know how sensitive a mother I am. I knew something was wrong with Fee Fee. I felt it right in my heart," Ma said as she balled her right hand into a fist and twisted the knuckles into her chest.

Aunt Jacqueline stood at the sink with her back to Ma, peeling and slicing sweet potatoes. She had her head cocked and was nodding and tsk-tsking Ma's story along. Aunt Jacqueline was definitely not dressed for an especially good or especially bad event. I think the blue and purple flowered dress she was wearing was intended to be ankle length. But Aunt Jacqueline, to put it nicely, is freakin' humongous. Aunt Merlude said that after eight children Aunt Jacqueline's body just got used to its pregnant size. After the dress made its way down and around her boobs, it took off on either side of her waist at an angle practically parallel to the floor, before dropping abruptly to sway a foot or so from each thigh. The backs of Aunt Jacqueline's dresses always hang shorter than the front ends because her butt sticks out like a round-edged shelf. That morning the dress that should have been ankle length barely covered the yellow-striped tube socks that she had pulled up to her knees. She was wearing those puffy-looking nurse's shoes, only they were brown instead of white. She topped off the entire outfit with a wide-brimmed black church hat that had a plastic red rose tucked in the band.

"I was going to call home, but the foreman came into the break room and told us it was time to go back to the floor," Ma continued. "That man—black as dirt—beat and beat my child and locked the others in the bathroom so they couldn't help her." Ma started to cry.

Aunt Jacqueline looked up at the ceiling and clapped her hands as if applauding. "Jesus, Jesus," she chanted over and over. When she stopped, she let out a loud breath, then flung her arms out and toward each other until she could grab her wrists. She rested her hands just under her boobs and started muttering to herself. It was her favorite stance. I could never tell if she was holding up her chest or holding down her stomach.

"He thinks he can kill my children?!" Ma said. "But what can I do? I can't stay home and watch them. In this country everyone must work."

Aunt Jacqueline shook her head, then finally dropped her gaze and returned to the sweet potatoes.

I backed up into the hallway and turned to the church ladies. They were still praying and singing with their eyes closed, as if they were so used to such vigils they could do them in their sleep. I snuck up between two of them and peeked into Aunt Merlude's room. That is the only thing I did all of that year that I regret doing. Truly.

Enid was laid out on the bed on her stomach. Her arms were stretched up beside her and doubled back at her elbows, so that her hands were on her head. She was gripping her hair real tight, like she was trying to either pull her hair out or hold her head down on the pillow. I thought I could hear her breathing even over the noise of the church ladies. Her breathing sounded like half snoring, half gargling. Enid was completely naked, and from her neck down to the backs of her knees there wasn't a patch on her that looked like the body of a normal human being.

Have you ever seen the packing bubbles they use to keep things like glass or plates from breaking in the mail? I guess that's the best way to describe what Enid's back looked like that morning. Only, the bubbles were all different sizes, and from where I stood, I knew they were filled with the hot, salty, tangy, clear goo that comes out of skin bubbles after you've been burned.

Yeah, I tasted it once after a pot of boiling water the Daddy threw at me burned my arm. Enid must have gotten burned when the Daddy knocked her back into the stove.

Some of Enid's bubbles had already popped—on purpose or accidentally, I had no idea and really didn't want to know. I still don't. The ones that were popped had lipstick-red raw patches of flesh showing through the torn slits. The rows made out of skin that hadn't bubbled over were dark purple and dark blue.

My grandmother was there that morning too. She was dressed pretty much like Aunt Jacqueline—brightly colored muumuu dress and tube socks—but she had on a long-sleeved sweater also, and she'd taken off her hat and placed it on the windowsill. She was squeezing a washcloth in a basin of soapy water, then tapping at Enid's back with it.

While the church ladies sang, Aunt Merlude stood praying near the foot of the bed with her arms in the air. She was bent slightly over, but with each breath she took before continuing her prayer, she would snap back briefly. It reminded me of Enid heaving in and out, squirming on the floor during her beat-up.

Aunt Merlude opened her eyes. The church ladies had stopped singing and were staring at me. Suddenly they began shaking their heads and frowning.

"*Cherie, cherie,*" one was calling. They started toward me and their heads began to grow enormously. I blinked once. They kept coming at me. I blinked again, and when I tried to back away, I realized I was on the floor in the hallway. Ma and Aunt Jacqueline came rushing out of the kitchen.

"What happened?" I heard Ma ask.

"I heard something go *thump*, and when we turned around, there she was," said a church lady.

"This isn't something a little girl should see," said another.

"No," a third agreed. "Especially not her sister."

The church ladies' heads disappeared, and Ma and Aunt Jacqueline were looking down at me.

"Why aren't you in bed?" Ma asked. I grunted.

"Come and help me outside, Katu," said Aunt Jacqueline as she grabbed my arm and pulled me off the floor. I glanced quickly into the bedroom. Gran was still tapping Enid's back with the washcloth. The church ladies squeezed themselves into the little room, and Aunt Merlude closed the door.

Aunt Jacqueline went out the front door and around to the backyard. The sun was just coming up, and I noticed that the Daddy's taxi wasn't in the driveway. When I caught up with her, Aunt Jacqueline was pulling branches thick with leaves off the bushes by the shed. I could hear the church ladies singing inside the house.

"Your mother is rich, Katu," she said. "She has everything she needs to make medicine right here in the backyard."

She held a fistful of green and brown stuff under my nose.

"Can you smell the medicine?" she asked. It smelled like grass and dirt to me, but I nodded anyway.

She made her way around the yard, plucking branches and leaves and stems of grass and making "hmm-hmm" and "whoa-whoa" sounds all the way. Some of what she collected she thrust into my hands; the rest she stuffed into a plastic grocery bag to take back to Brooklyn. There are no backyards with medicine grass in Brooklyn—only fat buildings and skinny houses all squished together around strips of concrete here and there to play hopscotch or jump rope on.

Finally Aunt Jacqueline made her way to the leg of our deck where a stand of grass grew as high up as my waist. I'd long since stopped wondering why the Daddy never trimmed the grass there, but that morning I found out.

"Look, look," Aunt Jacqueline said as she pulled up a handful of the grass. Again she held it up to my nose. This grass smelled different, almost lemony. I arched my brows. Aunt Jacqueline sighed loudly, then shredded a blade with her fingernails and held it up to my nose again. Honey and lemon. I took the blade from her and drew in a deep breath through my nose. Lemony honey. Before I could stop it, my tongue darted out and licked the rough blade. Aunt Jacqueline slapped me on my bare arm.

"You're not a baby," she said. "They have to be washed first."

When she turned to head up the steps of the deck, I grabbed a handful of the lemon-honey grass and stuffed it into my pocket.

Ma had pulled the telephone from the hallway into

the kitchen and sat at the table telling someone the Enid beat-up story. Her eyes were open as wide as they could go, and they were wet. The holes in her nose opened wide each time she stopped to take a breath. Every couple of sentences she would slam her hand on the table, *THWACK!*

"...locked all the kids in the bathroom. By the grace of God, the Great Master, King of All, they escaped!"

THWACK!

"Now my eldest is lying in this house near death! Even if she doesn't die, only God, the Great Master, King of All, knows if she'll ever walk again, if she'll ever sit again, if she'll ever be the same Fee Fee again!"

THWACK!

"If that man—black as dirt—tries to step back into this house again, I swear I'll call the police myself! Even if I have to take all my children and live on the street and beg for food, I promise God ..."

THWACK!

"... the Great Master ..."

THWACK!

"... King of All ..."

THWACK!

"... I'll see that man—black as dirt—in hell before I let him back here again!"

THWACK! THWACK! THWACK!

Aunt Jacqueline took two pots out of the cabinet. One she filled with water, the other with milk. She set them both to boil on the stovetop. In the pot of water she placed a handful of sugar and some of the leaves and stems I'd placed on the counter. In the pot of milk she dumped the sliced sweet potatoes and some salt. Then she took a handful of the lemon-honey grass she'd already run under water, tied one blade around the rest of the bunch, and put it in with the sweet potatoes and milk.

"Your mother has had a very big shock," Aunt Jacqueline said as she pulled a bottle of cooking oil from one of the cabinets. "Get me a large spoon."

She sprinkled some salt onto the spoon, then stood in front of Ma and added oil to the salted spoon. Ma stopped her story in midsentence, and Aunt Jacqueline popped the spoonful of oil and salt into her mouth. Ma scrunched up her face real tight, then swallowed and went back to her story.

Aunt Jacqueline then poured another spoonful of salt and oil and turned to me.

"Oh, no," I said as I backed away from her. "I'm not in shock."

She didn't reply, only stood there with the spoon stretched toward my mouth and gave me that look. You know the look adults give, that *The only choice is this or the belt* look. I opened my mouth, and she shoved the spoon in, nearly knocking out a couple of my teeth when she yanked the spoon back. The slime left a chalky feel on my teeth, and some of the oil felt like it was making its way up the back of my throat to exit out of my nose. I ran to the sink and started sucking cold water directly from the tap.

When I could drink no more, I stood up. My lips

were curled down as far as they could go, and I clenched my teeth hard, trying to keep from puking. Aunt Jacqueline had returned to the stove and was stirring the contents of the pots.

"Parents don't use belts on their kids in Haiti," she said without looking away from the stove. "They take dried leather and twist it into strips."

She turned suddenly and grabbed my arm.

"The marks the *reegwaz* makes are thin, long, and red," she explained as she pressed a ragged fingernail into the inside of my elbow and dragged it toward my wrist. I winced.

"Every slap with a *reegwaz* is like three from a belt. It hurts more when you get hit and stings for much longer afterward. But it doesn't kill our kids. Of course, kids in Haiti would never throw food away. They aren't spoiled like you Americans."

I yanked my arm out of her grip and ran into the hallway bathroom. I stood in front of the toilet with my legs parted wide and leaned an elbow onto the tank. I stuck the index finger of my other hand as far into my throat as it would go and puked up oil and water. It's a weight-loss trick Enid uses, but I wasn't trying to lose weight. If the cooking oil was supposed to calm me down and make me sorry that the poor Daddy didn't have the proper weapon to beat us with, then I preferred to be in shock.

6.

I found myself alone in my bedroom when I awoke later that Saturday. I was soaking wet with sweat. The air conditioner had been turned off, and nobody had bothered to open my window. I stripped off my pants and shirt and put on a nightgown—it was daylight out, but I didn't think I'd be going anywhere the rest of the day. I noticed that the Daddy's taxi was still not in the driveway when I opened the window. I heard no noise from downstairs and wondered where everyone was. Then I remembered Augustin. You do know about Augustin, don't you? No? Then, why do you look so freaked out? Sorry, I didn't mean to laugh at you.

Anyway, back then it was my job to bring Augustin his dinner. On weekends it was breakfast, lunch, and dinner. Augustin was the only Haitian person I knew who didn't go to work at all on weekends. He spent most of his time in the room he rented in our basement, sitting at the sewing machine making dresses and pants and bedspreads and curtains. The little radio he had was always tuned to a Haitian news and music station broadcasting from Brooklyn.

Ma said men like Augustin didn't really exist—that

she sometimes thought the stories about him being a zombie were true. All because he was real quiet and went only to work and to church and to the little office in the back of the Haitian bakery on Main Street, where he sent all the extra money he had to his wife and son in Haiti. He didn't drink. He didn't smoke. He didn't curse. He didn't go to parties. And he didn't have a girlfriend.

See, supposedly Augustin is on his second lifetime. His first ended back in Haiti when a woman jealous that he had married someone else put a curse on him and he fell into a coma and died. His family held a wake for him, and the burial was to be the day after, but when the funeral home guys opened up the next morning, they found his coffin empty. The funeral home owners got beaten up pretty badly for not properly securing the coffin and the building. After all, it was Haiti and it wasn't like disappearing corpses were a new thing to anyone. They should have known better.

No one knows how, but Augustin showed up three years later in New York. He and the Daddy used to be childhood friends, and they reconnected when Augustin showed up here. That's how he ended up in our basement. Ma wasn't too thrilled with renting a room to a dead guy, but the Daddy insisted, and it turned out that this dead guy was pretty cool. Paid his rent on time, loved Ma's cooking, and didn't hit on Enid or bring strange women in and out of the house. All around, Augustin was much better tenant than the live ones we'd had before him.

I managed to make my way to the basement without being seen by anyone. Delta and the twins and the babies were hanging out on the back porch. I didn't see or hear anyone else. I figured Ma had gone into the factory for some overtime. Augustin was at his sewing machine as usual. He stopped his work completely when I walked in. That was different. He held his arm out to me.

"Katu, *comment ça va?*" he asked. He looked worried.

"I'm fine," I said after planting a kiss on his cheek.

Augustin was just as dark skinned as the Daddy, but I never heard Ma call him black as dirt. I never heard Ma say anything bad about Augustin.

He blew out a breath and squeezed my arm.

"Did you eat today?" I asked.

"*Oui.*"

"Delta brought you lunch?"

"*Oui.*"

"Did you see Enid?"

He shook his head slowly and blew out a breath again.

"I tried to save her," I said as he let my arm go and reached over to turn off the radio. "I gave her CPR. You know, breathed in her mouth? They showed us how in school. I got her to start breathing again, but she wouldn't wake up. So I ran and got Uncle Jude."

"Jude?" he asked.

"Yeah."

He looked up toward the stairs and made a face like he was trying to listen through the ceiling.

"Uncle Jude is not here now," I explained.

Augustin just nodded, then patted the corner of his bed. I sat down, and he turned back to his sewing machine. Augustin was attaching a giant bow to the back of a long lime green dress. The dress was obviously for a bridesmaid. There were already three others just like it hanging on the roll-away clothes rack that stood in the corner. Just looking at the lace around the neck and at the wrists made me itchy. I had heard Ma talking about someone getting married and hoped one of the dresses wasn't for me. I didn't think it was. Augustin hadn't measured us in a long time.

"I think Daddy is going to kill one of us one day," I said.

Augustin nodded but didn't look up.

"Maybe we should run away," I shouted over the buzzing of the sewing machine. "Or call the police."

"Police here?" Augustin lifted his foot off the pedal and the sewing machine stopped. He looked at me wide eyed.

"No, no," I said. "I said *maybe* we should call the police."

"Oh."

"You think we should call the police?"

He shook his head.

I reached behind me and pulled down the picture of Augustin's son off the shelf above his bed. Marcus would be his name if he ever came to America, only Augustin pronounced it "Ma-kiss." Marcus was about four years old in the picture. He sat on a white wicker chair. Behind him were all kinds of beautiful plants and trees. In the distance you could see a mountain. But the plants and trees and the mountain weren't real. They were painted onto a screen like the kind they rolled into our classroom to show movies. I could see one edge of the screen, and right behind it was wood paneling. I wondered why they had to use a fake background when they lived on a real-life island.

I also wondered if Augustin would ever give Marcus a beat-up if he did something wrong. I never bothered asking 'cause Augustin and Marcus had never met each other. Marcus was born after Augustin had died and disappeared. I don't think Augustin would ever hit him, though. Ma is right. He's nothing like a real Haitian guy.

"Guess what?" I said. "I have a new best friend."

Augustin tore a piece of green thread with his teeth.

"Her name is Suzanne, and she's the prettiest girl in school. We're going to be pen pals this summer."

I put Marcus's picture back on the shelf and picked up the Polaroid camera next to it. Augustin took pictures at every fitting he did to help him adjust the dresses until they were perfect. I'd never like wearing frilly-girl dresses, but at least Augustin made us laugh when he'd point his camera at us and get us to yell, *"Fromage, fromage, fromage!"*

"Do you ever write letters to Marcus?" I asked as I pointed the camera at him.

Augustin nodded and smiled. Augustin had the

most amazing smile. You could see practically all of his teeth when he smiled. They were absolutely the whitest and biggest teeth of anyone I knew. It seemed like I was staring into Augustin's teeth through the camera lens for a while, watching him nod and smile. By the time I heard Gran calling me, she was screeching— somewhere between frantic and pissed off. I'd almost forgotten she was in the house. I pushed the button on the camera and nothing happened. Augustin reached into a bag on his desk and pulled out two new boxes of camera film. *"Fromage,"* he whispered as Gran continued to scream out my name. I tossed the camera onto his bed and ran up the stairs.

My grandmother doesn't speak a lick of English even though she's lived in New York since before I was born. Gran and Aunt Jacqueline are more like sisters than mother and daughter, and they don't get along at all, but they live together. My cousin Edner says that's because Haitian people like to torture themselves. They're so used to being miserable that whenever they aren't, they have to go find something to be miserable about. He says that's why Aunt Jacqueline—that's his mom—went and got Gran from Haiti. After Aunt Jacqueline's first husband died, she didn't have anyone to fight with except her kids, and that wasn't enough.

Gran was heading back into Aunt Merlude's room when I got upstairs. I didn't want to follow her in. I wanted to make sure Enid was okay, but I didn't want to see her naked back again. I stood in the hallway and called, "Gran?"

She came out of the bedroom with dollars in her hand and stood looking at me. "Have you seen me yet since I've been here?" she asked in Creole.

I shook my head.

"I know you're American, but you're Haitian, too. Don't forget your manners."

I walked over and kissed her on the cheek.

"Go to the pharmacy," she said as she handed me the money. "Get rubbing alcohol and big Band-Aids."

"*Oui*, Gran," I answered, and took a quick look into the bedroom. Enid was still on her stomach, but she was covered with a sheet.

"She is not going to die," Gran said. I nodded and went to my room to change.

The quickest way to get to the pharmacy is to cross the street from our house and then turn the corner at Mr. Hollings's house, then go down a block and turn left. But I could see that Mr. Hollings was in his front yard, so I stayed on our side of the street, passed Alaska Street, and went up another block and turned right. I pretended not to see Mr. Hollings, but out of the corner of my eye I saw him wave to me.

Mr. Hollings is a total perv. I feel really bad for his daughter 'cause everyone on the block and everyone at school knows her dad is a perv who likes to touch kids. They make fun of her at school because of it. Like it's not bad enough she has the worst buckteeth in the history of the world and gets called Rabbit Face, but she also has to have a pervert for a father.

Mr. Hollings put the moves on me once, but I never

told anyone. Ma would have killed me if she found out I got into his car. Actually, I got into his car twice. I didn't have much of a choice, though. Once in fourth grade and then again in fifth grade I let him take me to school when I had missed the bus. It was either go home and get a beat-up for missing the bus before being taken to school, or walk to school and get a beat-up after school for bringing home a tardy note, or let Mr. Hollings drive me.

Mr. Hollings always knows when someone misses the bus, because the bus stop is at the corner at the side of his house. The first time, when I was in fourth grade, when I came running around the corner and found no one waiting there, not even dumb old Delta, who was always missing the school bus, Mr. Hollings was clipping the bushes near his sidewalk.

"Just missed it, little lady, heh-heh-heh." Yeah, like a ten-year-old missing the school bus was the funniest joke ever. So funny I forgot to laugh.

"Guess your ma'll have to take you, heh-heh-heh."

I looked up and down the street. No one else was around. The middle school kids wouldn't be coming out for their bus for almost another hour.

"I'll just walk," I mumbled, and started toward Memorial.

Before I had reached Memorial Avenue, Mr. Hollings pulled up next to me and rolled down his window.

"I can give you a ride if you'd like, little lady, heh-heh."

"That's okay," I said. But I stopped walking.

"Well, I'm heading that way anyhow. Gotta buy a new rake at Mason's Hardware."

Then he looked at his watch and said, "You'll miss the first bell. Especially at the rate you're walking, heh-heh-heh."

He reached over and unlocked the passenger door. He pushed the door open so hard it nearly knocked me over. I got in real quick before I could change my mind. Before I even closed the door, though, I grabbed the seat belt and buckled myself in. Delta had made the mistake of letting Mr. Hollings help her with the seat belt when she chose to get a ride to school instead of getting a beat-up. When she told me what had happened, I said that I would tell Ma. But Delta cried and shook and dug her nails into my arms and made me swear never to tell. Eventually I promised I wouldn't, but only after I'd made her swear she'd never get in the car with him again. Besides, I figured that if I just buckled myself in, then he'd have no reason to reach over to *help* me, if you know what I mean, and I wouldn't have the same problem Delta did. So I buckled up first, then closed the car door, then hugged my backpack to my chest, then crossed my right leg over my left knee and then under my left leg again. I was holding them together so tight that by the time I got to school, I almost couldn't feel my feet. When I took a ride to school from Mr. Hollings in the fifth grade, I got smarter. I rode in the backseat. He didn't find much to heh-heh-heh about that second time.

Anyway, the whole way to the pharmacy I was

fantasizing about what life would be like without the Daddy. First thing for sure, I'd get Ma to let me invite friends over the house. Well, yeah, I'd actually have to make friends first, but I could work on that. I'd start with Suzanne Ryan. She'd come over and we'd pretend to do homework together, only we'd really just listen to the radio and dance around my room.

After school we wouldn't have to hurry up to stuff our faces. We'd eat as slow as we pleased and maybe even watch television while we ate. The boys would always have chores to do, and they couldn't stall and stall until the Daddy came home, because he wouldn't be coming home. We'd get Ma to see that the Haitian way of treating boys and girls just wouldn't work any-more. "You're gonna handicap them for life, Ma," Enid would say. "If boys aren't taught how to cook and clean for themselves, they're going to suffer. Women in this country don't do those things for men anymore." And Ma would look at Roland and Gerald and the twins and think about the Daddy out there somewhere trying to fend for himself, when he needed help just to heat up food that had already been cooked for him, and she'd sigh and say, "You right. Go wash the dishes, Joseph."

Ma might still yell at us when we pissed her off, but no one would ever again get a beat-up. I got so caught up in our new lives that I didn't hear the pharmacy cashier until he was practically yelling.

"Eighteen cents, miss!"

He was holding the three crumpled dollars I must have handed to him and was leaning over the counter.

"The total is three eighteen," he said.

I searched my pockets like I just knew I had more money somewhere.

"Which do you want to put back?" asked the cashier as he held up the bottle of rubbing alcohol and the box of bandages.

"Both," I said, and grabbed the dollar bills out of his hand. What a jerk. Eighteen lousy cents and he didn't even offer to let me bring it next time. I was buying rubbing alcohol and bandages, not Snickers bars and bubble gum. Wasn't it obvious it was an emergency? I walked out to the sidewalk and didn't even bother starting back home.

Uncle Jude seemed really surprised to see me. His eyes were red, but I didn't smell any alcohol. When I told him what I needed, he said, "Wait one little minute," and closed the door without letting me into his apartment.

He was back before I could think of what would make him act so funny. He handed me a five-dollar bill and said, "I come later, okay, sweetheart?"

It wasn't until I was walking back to the pharmacy that I noticed the Daddy's taxi parked in the far corner of Uncle Jude's lot.

7.

I stood in the hallway listening to Enid moan and cry as Gran rubbed her down with the alcohol I'd bought. Gran stepped out into the hallway and was headed to the kitchen when she noticed me.

"Wait, Katu," she said. She went back into the bedroom, and as I entered behind her, I realized she'd gone back to cover Enid. I guess she was afraid I'd faint again if I saw Enid's back. She was probably right. When Gran left the room, I brought out a bag from behind my back and held it near Enid's head. She was staring at the wall, away from me. I shook the bag and she turned her head slowly.

On the way out of the shopping center I'd stopped into the kosher deli and bought four potato knishes. I knelt down in front of Enid and pulled one out of the bag.

"Want one?" I asked.

Delta hates knishes, but Enid loves them as much as I do. She hadn't been eating them much anymore because of her diet, but when she did have one, she didn't puke it up right away like she did with other food.

"Mustard?" Enid asked. Her voice was a hoarse whisper.

"Of course," I said. The only way I eat a knish is by smearing mustard on the outside and then sprinkling salt on top of the mustard. Enid skips the salt. I'd eat knishes all day long if I could afford to or knew how to make them.

I handed Enid a knish with mustard, and she started eating it without lifting her head off her pillow.

"You eat anything since last night?" I asked.

"A little bit of soup and some tea."

"Tea they made with grass stuff?"

"Yeah."

I pulled the blades of grass out of my pocket and handed them to her. "Like this?" I asked. Enid nodded.

"Yuck," I said.

"Actually, this isn't too bad," said Enid. "It's lemongrass. Kinda smells like our shampoo."

I took the blades back and smelled them again. "Hey, you're right! I hadn't noticed before. Lemongrass and honey. Smells like our hair grease too."

I didn't know what else to say. I felt so bad for her. Her face was still puffy and all different colors. She'd been cleaned up pretty good, but I could still see a crust of dried blood at the corner of her nose. We ate the rest of the knishes without speaking.

Delta walked in and wrinkled her nose at the sight and smell of knishes, then sat down next to me. It was then that I remembered Ma's telephone conversation.

"Guess what?" I said. "Ma said that if Daddy tries to come back home, she's going to call the police."

"She said that to him?" asked Delta.

"No, she was talking to someone on the telephone. But I think she really means it this time."

Delta looked at Enid and then looked away.

"You know what, Fee Fee?" An idea had just popped into my head, so clear as day I wondered why I'd never considered it in all the years the Daddy had been pounding on us. "We all should make a pact and swear that when we get married, we'll never let our husbands treat our kids like Daddy does. We should prick our fingers and press them together and become blood sisters and swear."

"We're already sisters, Katu," said Enid.

"Oh, yeah, I know," I said. "But we should swear anyway."

"How would we ever stop someone like Daddy?" Delta asked.

I shrugged. "It's just an idea."

Enid shifted in the bed so that her arm stretched out toward the floor. She winced and closed her eyes briefly. Opening her eyes again, she placed her hand on my knee and made a pathetic attempt at squeezing it. Her wrist was swollen and beet colored. Her pinkie stuck straight out at a weird angle, like my knee was a cup of fancy tea and she was about to take a sip.

"I think that's a very good idea, Katu," whispered Enid.

It was all the encouragement I needed. "All you'd have to do is call for help. We could have a signal, like . . . like . . ."

"Like 'The eagle has landed,'" said Enid.

"No!" yelled Delta as she jumped up suddenly and began twirling around and flapping her arms like a bird. "'Your guardian angel has landed'!"

"Yeah, something like that," I continued. "Then we'd sneak into your house in the middle of the night." I got up and tiptoed around the tiny room. "Crawl through a window . . ."

"I'd leave the front door unlocked," said Enid. "Your wings might not fit through a window."

"Then we'd find the rotten bastard and . . . and . . ." I started shadowboxing and throwing myself around. "We'd stomp on him and kick him and punch him in the privates! Then I'd grab his head and bang, bang, bang it against the wall and . . ." I realized suddenly that the room had gone quiet. I turned back to Enid's bed. She had both hands covering her eyes. She was gritting her teeth.

"Or we could raise our wings real wide over him and say a prayer and make him disappear," Delta said calmly.

I sat down again. Delta and I watched Enid nervously. Reenacting the violence Enid had just experienced wasn't the brightest idea we'd ever had, and we knew it. But after a few minutes of listening to our hearts thump, good ole Enid uncovered her eyes and came to our rescue.

"That sounds more like a witch than an angel, Dee Dee," she said.

"Dee Dee can be the chanting witch angel. But we're still gonna need a butt-kicking angel," I said quietly.

"Anyway, I think Ma's serious this time about not letting him back. You should have heard how mad she was on the phone."

Delta mumbled, "So she'll call the cops and then Daddy will go to jail and then we'll have to go on welfare and then—"

"It's not true, Dee Dee," said Enid.

"What?" Delta turned to look at Enid.

Enid coughed and cleared her throat and spoke louder. "It's not true about welfare and college."

Ma always said if a family got welfare, then the government wouldn't let their kids go to college. Everyone in Haiti knew that, she said. That's why people in our family came over and lived with one another for years, cramped into tiny apartments in Brooklyn, and worked two or three jobs. They figured they could afford a nicer place after the kids went to college and got good jobs. And worse still, Ma swore that all the poor kids on welfare ended up in special-ed classes and could never work at sit-down jobs.

Enid and I weren't so worried about not going to college. But Delta was the smart one, and for as long as I could remember, all she'd talked about was going to Harvard. She didn't know what she wanted to be when she grew up, but she figured since Harvard was the best college in the world, if she went there, then she could do whatever she wanted once she figured it out.

One day the Daddy had heard us saying something about Boston and realized that Harvard was not the community college in the county. He said that girls didn't leave home until they were married, and that after high school Delta could go to the community college or maybe a college in the city and come home every day, where a Haitian girl belonged. Ma agreed.

We might not have known that the welfare and college thing wasn't true, but at least we knew that once you turned eighteen, then your parents couldn't tell you what to do. So Delta stopped talking about Harvard after Enid and I told her not to worry. If she got into Harvard and Ma disowned her, then Enid and I would get extra jobs and send money to help her pay for books and stuff.

Now, if what Enid was saying was true, then maybe we could get out from under the Daddy and not end up dirt poor on the street and Delta could still go to college.

"My boy—I have a friend who's moving to Boston in September to be near his sister, and—"

"You have a boyfriend?" Delta interrupted Enid.

"No, I don't, Dee Dee. What I was saying was . . ." Enid shifted and winced again. "My friend's sister got into Harvard, and their whole family's on welfare," she said.

Delta and I looked at each other.

"Are you sure, Fee Fee?" asked Delta.

Enid nodded.

"I mean about being on welfare and going to college."

"Positive," said Enid.

"Like, totally, totally positive?" Delta was standing now and getting way too excited.

Enid nodded again.

"We should tell Ma!"

"Don't bother," Enid said.

"Why not?" I asked. If Ma knew about this, then maybe next time she really would call the police.

"It's not like you get rich when you get welfare, you know," said Enid.

"I know that," said Delta.

"There are rules, too," Enid said. "We'll probably have to move into an apartment in the projects, and they won't let Aunt Merlude or the twins or Augustin come with us."

I said, "Maybe they can give Aunt Merlude an apartment too, and Augustin can rent a room anywhere. He's the nicest guy."

"I forgot about Aunt Merlude," said Delta. She wasn't excited anymore. She sat back down on the floor Indian style and put her head in her hands.

"What's wrong?" I asked.

"They'll send Aunt Merlude and the twins back to Haiti if they find out about them," Enid said.

"What are you talking about?" I asked. Delta seemed to know just what Enid was talking about, and it was beginning to piss me off.

"How could you be so clueless, Katu?" asked Delta. "Aunt Merlude and Jack and Joseph aren't supposed to be here."

"In our house?"

"In the country."

"Why the hell not?"

Then Enid sighed and said, "Katu, they were only supposed to come for a couple of months for vacation and then go back to Haiti. That's all the government would give them permission for."

"But they've been here way longer than two months," I said.

"Duh," said Delta.

"Wait," I said. I thought I was starting to clue in to some things. "What about Augustin?"

"Augustin Noel is legally dead," said Enid. "We call the guy downstairs Augustin, but when he came to this country, he came as Jean Bassett."

I'd heard that name before. "Remember how mad Ma got that time you wrote 'wrong address' on the mail that had 'Jean Bassett' on it?" asked Delta.

"How do you guys know all this stuff?" I asked.

"You'd know too," said Delta, "if you ever stopped daydreaming and making up stories and paid attention to the real world."

"But Ma is allowed to be here, right?" I was beginning to feel sick. "I mean, she's a citizen for real, right?"

She must have been. I remembered her studying for her citizenship test. I remembered her mumbling around the house as she cooked or cleaned, "George Washington is first president, ten bill of right, freedom speech, freedom religion . . ." And I remembered the day sometime after the wedding when we all went to some big auditorium filled with people holding tiny American flags, and Ma raised her hand with everyone else and said a bunch of stuff, and then everyone clapped and some people cried and then the man on the stage said, "Welcome, my fellow American citizens," and then gave a long, boring speech.

"Yup," said Enid. "Thanks to you."

"Me?" I asked. Delta looked at Enid too. Maybe this part she didn't know about either.

"Ma could have waited forever to become a citizen, or she could just pop out a baby and do it that way," said Enid.

"They let you become a citizen just for having a baby?" I asked. Did New York have some kind of baby shortage I didn't know about?

"Oh," said Delta, who as usual caught on before I did. "'Cause you're automatically a citizen if you're born here, so they're not gonna send back a mother who just had an American baby, 'cause then who would take care of it? Right, Fee Fee?"

Enid nodded and said, "So that's how Ma got to be a citizen."

I didn't know if I should be proud or ashamed. My ears started to burn and I felt dizzy.

"Why are you raising your hand, Katu?" asked Delta.

"Oh, not again," I heard Enid say.

"Can't . . . breathe," I managed to let out before falling back on the floor.

8.

Ma went about trying to make life without the Daddy work right from the beginning. She picked up so many extra shifts at the factory we barely saw her at all those first few weeks. But Ma always managed to make it home early on Saturday afternoons, and she and Gran and Aunt Merlude would gather in the kitchen to cook and talk and talk.

On one of those Saturdays, Enid was in what became her usual spot that summer—a busted-up beach chair on the back porch. She lay stretched out with a book in her lap. Delta and I were trying to teach the boys how to play hide-and-seek, but there were only so many places to hide, since we weren't allowed to let them out of the backyard. I squinted my eyes, and as I watched Jack drag Roland underneath the porch, Enid crooked her finger at me.

"Ready or not, here I come!" I yelled.

I walked a slow circle around the yard, then tiptoed up the porch steps, pretending hard not to see Joseph with his back pressed up against the side of the house and his head poking around the corner. Enid continued waggling her finger at me until I was kneeling beside her. She pointed to the open page in the book and whispered, "Listen."

"Listen to what?" I asked, staring at the page.

Enid shifted her eyes toward the kitchen without moving her head, and I caught on. Enid was eavesdropping on the conversation going on in the kitchen. It was pretty great stuff we heard. Ma, Gran, and Aunt Merlude were going on and on about the Daddy. Gaston was a rotten bastard. Living with Gaston was worse than packing up the kids and going to live in a shack in Haiti. The Gaston bashing had been going on most Saturday nights, and it always made me tingly. It seemed to rev Ma up too.

It started to rain before I could return to the yard and pretend to look for everyone. We ended up roller-skating in the hallway between the living room and Aunt Merlude's bedroom. Delta and I took turns sharing our skates with the twins. My roller skates were a bit too big for their feet and Delta's were a bit too small, and they couldn't skate, but the twins didn't care. I stood at the edge of the living room and gave Jack a shove down the hallway, where Delta waited with open arms to catch him. His hands high in the air, Jack switched his hip like a belly dancer to avoid Joseph, who was crawling on his hands and knees toward me for his turn, and missed Delta's arms by a mile. He crashed into the wall nose-first and slid down to the floor.

"Who's tearing down the house?" Gran shouted from the kitchen.

"Nobody!" Delta and I yelled back.

Ma came out to the hallway as Jack pulled up to his knees and shook himself like a wet dog. She looked first at Jack, then at me. You should have seen me smiling like a goof. Normally something like this would end up with us getting a beat-up. But between all the extra hours Ma was putting in at the factory and the Saturday-night girl powwows with Aunt Merlude and Gran, she'd loosened up quite a bit about our behavior. It was as if we'd taken a vacation to Uncle Jude's place, only without the booze and the dirty channels on cable television.

Ma shook her head at me, started back for the kitchen, then changed her mind. "Dee Dee," she said.

"Yes, Ma?" answered Delta.

"Any big university you want," said Ma. "You cannot depend on men in this life."

"Okay," Delta barely choked out as Ma turned on her heel and went back into the kitchen.

Aunt Merlude had stopped tossing chicken legs into the metal mixing bowl to coat them with spices and hot sauce. Gran stopped snipping the ends off of a paper bag full of green beans with her fingernails. Ma's shadow lay still on the hallway floor. Then, after we'd been holding our breaths for a while, came "Humph" from the kitchen. That was Gran. Aunt Merlude followed with, "Do you hear what she is saying to that girl?"

I understood what was going on then, and ran over to take it out on Jack. "It's my turn!" I yelled at him, then yanked the skates off his feet wihout untying the laces.

I avoided looking at Delta. If I could figure out that Gran and Aunt Merlude expected Gaston's exile to be simply a long punishment and not a forever punishment, then she had figured it out five seconds before I had.

The next Saturday afternoon I heard Aunt Merlude comment on how much weight Ma was losing. "How much longer can you work so hard?" she asked. Later it was Gran who suggested that maybe the problem with Gaston was that the girls needed better training, and she asked, "Why do they have to be told over and over again how to behave?" Ma was mostly quiet. Uncle Jude joined Ma and Gran and Aunt Merlude in the kitchen most Saturday nights but never said a word about the Daddy that I could hear. The more air that leaked out of Ma's bubble, the more time Uncle Jude spent sitting at the table with his head in his hand.

9.

I got tired of playing quicksand. Delta said she was tired of it too, but she was lying. She liked jumping from the beds to the dresser and stuff just as much as Gerald and the twins did. We weren't allowed to remove Gerald's braces for no good reason, but I felt sorry for him when he couldn't play quicksand with us. Besides, it seemed that hopping and jumping on furniture was a lot easier for him than walking on the floor.

I wanted to play gin rummy, but Delta suggested go fish so everyone could play. She was looking at Enid, but Enid didn't uncurl herself or even open her eyes. She just lay there on her side with one arm wrapped around Roland, who was sitting propped up against her. The twins wanted to play war, which is the dumbest card game ever invented by mankind, plus they still wanted to play quicksand. I told Delta to go ahead and get the cards. They were somewhere in the kitchen. We'd play go fish, but the floor of the bedroom was still quicksand.

Delta hopped from the bed to a chair we had brought up from the kitchen, then pulled herself into a sitting position on the dresser. She leaned over, opened the door, and jumped out into the hallway, landing on her hands and knees. The twins jumped up and down on the bed, clapping their hands.

"Are you ever going to do anything with us anymore?" I asked Enid. She knew I was talking to her because I was holding one of her eyelids open.

"I have cramps," she whispered as she pushed my hand away.

"Oh," I said. It had been three weeks since her beatup, and though she still slept downstairs with Aunt Merlude, Enid did try to hang out with us some. She was still in a lot of pain most of the time, I could tell. It wasn't just monthly cramps. She limped, too. And the limp didn't seem to be getting any better.

I didn't hear the doorbell ring, but it must have. Delta came pounding up the steps and ran into the room, slamming the door behind her. She didn't walk on the furniture. Joseph and Jack started squealing, "Queesan'! Queesan'! You dead, Dee Dee!"

Delta ignored them. She was breathing hard and her eyes were opened so wide I thought her eyeballs would pop out.

"There's a white lady downstairs and two policemen." She was tapping Enid's shoulders as she said this, but she was looking at me. Enid sat up too fast, jerked her arm toward her side in pain, and nearly knocked Roland off the bed.

"What did they say?" Enid asked.

"I don't know," said Delta.

The twins sensed something was wrong, and they

finally stopped yelling "Queesan'!" We tiptoed to the door and opened it. Enid turned out the light in the room. I could see the light coming from downstairs, but I couldn't hear much of anything above the rain and thunder outside. Every once in a while the lightning would light up our bedroom and I could see Enid chewing her thumbnail.

"Where are you all?" Ma yelled in Creole from the bottom of the stairs.

"We're up here," Enid answered. None of us moved.

"Come down now," Ma said a little quieter.

Enid and Delta and I went down the stairs. The twins stayed behind with Gerald and Roland. Ma looked at us like we'd done something wrong. Her hands were on her hips, her head was shaking. She stared at us all a second, then walked into the kitchen. We followed her in.

The white lady was grinning at us like we'd won a prize and she couldn't wait to give it to us. She was real skinny and young and pretty, with red hair in a big ole bun at the back of her neck. The two policemen didn't look happy at all. One of them had his hand on his nightstick like he was ready to whip it out any second. I wondered who he thought deserved a beat-up.

"Hi," said the white lady. "I hope we haven't disturbed y'all tonight."

Y'all? She sounded like the people on the television show *Dallas*. Maybe that's where she was from.

We didn't answer her. I think the grown-ups in the room were the only ones breathing right then.

"Well then," said the white lady. She looked inside

a folder she was carrying, then looked up right at Enid and asked, "Which one of y'all is Enid?"

Enid nodded.

"My name is Clara, Enid, and I'm a social worker with the county," she said real slowly. "Do you know what a social worker is?"

Enid nodded politely, but I could see her eyebrows twitching. Was the social worker there because someone had called about child abuse or child stupidity? Like, who doesn't know what a social worker is?

"Well then," Clara the social worker with the county said again. She was still grinning. "We have received a report that somebody has hurt you. Is that true?"

Enid looked at Ma hopefully. Ma put her hands back on her hips and gave Enid an *I dare you to tell them the truth* stare. It was a real quick stare, over before Enid could even blink. It was just that one quick stare that let us know Ma had once again lost her nerve about keeping the Daddy out of the house.

Enid looked at Clara and shook her head.

"Do you mind if I take a look-see at your back, honey?"

"No!" Enid shouted as she took a step backward.

The policeman with his hand on his stick stepped forward. "The lady just wants to make sure you're okay," he said, and walked toward Enid. Enid kept stepping back until she was almost out of the kitchen. "If you're okay, we can all get out of here and leave you alone."

Clara walked over to the policeman and put her hand on his elbow. "Let me," she said to him. Then to

Enid she said, "Why don't just you and me go out here to the hallway, okay?" Everything Clara said sounded like a question that wasn't really a question. She put her arm around Enid and led her to the hallway. Clara came back pretty quickly, and she wasn't grinning anymore. Enid didn't come back into the kitchen.

"Ma'am, you said that Enid was fighting with her sister?"

"They fight sometime," said Ma. "Kids always fight sometime." Then Ma looked at me. I didn't look at her. I didn't need a stare from Ma to know what she expected me to say.

"Is that how your sister got hurt?" Clara asked me.

"Yeah," I said without skipping a beat.

"What's that?" she asked.

"Yes!" I said louder.

"What were y'all fighting about?"

"Chores," I said. It wasn't a complete lie. No one said anything for a minute, so then I said, "She promised to do my chore and then she changed her mind, so I got mad and we got into a fight and she hit me and I hit her back and it was just a stupid fight and . . ."

"And?" asked Clara.

"Am I going to jail?" I asked Clara, but I was staring at the nightstick.

Clara looked at the policeman, who then looked at me and coughed and said, "Not this time."

Just then Jack walked into the kitchen with Roland on his hip. "Ti Wo Wo has sheet in his Pampers," said Jack. The policeman with the nightstick shook his head, and the other one looked like he was trying not to laugh.

"Go back up there!" Ma yelled, startling Jack so badly he almost dropped Roland.

Clara turned to Ma again as Jack left the kitchen. "Ma'am, your daughter needs to see a doctor for the bruises on her back."

"We don't have doctor," Ma said.

"There are several county clinics that will take care of her. For free."

"I take care of her," Ma said. Then she walked out of the kitchen and headed to the front door.

"There is a clinic not far from here on Main Street," Clara said to Ma's back. Clara hadn't moved, but the policemen followed Ma to the door.

Clara looked at me, and I looked right back at her, stared her right in the eye. I tried to do Ma's evil eye on her, but I wasn't feeling so evil then, at least not toward Clara the social worker. I blinked before she did, so I turned my evil eye to the floor.

As Clara passed me, she put her hand on my shoulder and said, "Everything'll be all right, honey."

After Clara and the policemen left, Ma came back into the kitchen and said that she needed to talk to us. There's something you have to know about Ma and her talks. She speaks English with us only when she's really happy—which is, like, never—or when she's too tired to give us beat-ups when we deserve it, so she begs us to be good as a favor to her so that her life can be a little less miserable than it usually is. And on those occasions she whines a lot and calls us "sweet-heart," like Uncle Jude does. That night, though, she wasn't happy at all, and she wasn't whining and calling us "sweetheart." But she was speaking English.

"Listen to me, Karina," Ma said.

There had been too many things that had happened for the first time after Enid's beat-up, and it was weird-ing me out. The Daddy had disappeared. Ma had to have strange people pick her up for work and bring her back home again. My grandmother had settled in like she'd never be leaving. She was doing most of our chores, and Ma didn't even complain about it. None of us kids had gotten a beat-up in weeks. Cops had shown up at our house and I had almost gone to jail. Now Ma was sitting in the kitchen speaking English and calling me Karina instead of Katu. I felt dizzy and wanted to throw up.

"Do you know what will happen if Gaston goes to jail?" Ma asked.

Delta can stop sleeping in the closet? We won't be afraid to come home from school? Augustin can be our new stepfather?

"You won't be able to pay the bills?" I answered.

"You very, very smart girl," Ma said. "And if I don't pay bills, what will happen?"

"We'll have no lights and no telephone like Uncle Jude sometimes?"

Ma nodded. "And what happen when the social worker find out I leave my children in the dark with no telephone and no air conditioner and no food?"

That one stumped me but not Delta.

"My friend Bella had to go to foster care because her mom was poor," she said.

"Do you want to go to foster care, Karina?" Ma asked.

"Can we all go together?" I asked.

Ma sat back in her chair, closed her eyes, and swallowed hard.

"I mean, can you come too . . . and the twins and Aunt Merlude . . . and Augustin?"

"Only kids get put in foster care, stupid," said Delta.

Ma was rubbing her forehead. "I told Gaston, he can't touch the girls anymore," Ma said. With her eyes still closed and her voice low, it was as if she were talking to herself. "No more beat-ups for the girls. They not yours."

Delta and I looked at each other. Ma was trying to tell us that the Daddy wasn't allowed to beat us, so everything would be just fine if he came back home. We had believed it the first time Ma made that deal, after the beat-up that Delta got where I almost called 911. Ma had tried that deal with the Daddy a couple more times after that. We didn't buy it anymore. But Ma seemed to *need* to believe it, and what could we say? The quiet made her open her eyes finally, and she stood up.

"Karina," she said loudly. "You bring police to my house again and I will give you a beat-up."

"But I didn't call them, Ma, I swear!"

She ignored that and said, "And you don't fight with your sister anymore. Fight again and I will give you a beat-up. You understand that?"

I did understand. I understood that I didn't want to

defend myself anymore. I wanted to defend Ma. I wanted to tell her not to feel so bad. It was okay that she had gone back on her word again about leaving the Daddy for good. It was okay because we all did it, you know. No matter how many times I sat in the purple chair and swore I'd be a better student, eventually I'd stop doing my homework. No matter how many times Enid promised not to act like the Daddy and go crazy with the belt when we upset her, it was like she couldn't help herself. It was like none of us could help going back to what we were used to, no matter how bad it was. But maybe next time would be different, I wanted to tell Ma. Just maybe we'd all get it right before it was too late.

A couple of days after I was told that I had beaten Enid, Father Sanon from church came over with a white man named Mr. Levinson and told us that the Daddy was in jail. Ma screamed and cried and slapped at her head.

"Tell us what happened that night, Karina," said Father Sanon.

We sat around the kitchen table, me and Delta and Ma and Father Sanon and Mr. Levinson. Enid had disappeared somewhere in the house as soon as she heard Father Sanon's voice at the front door.

"I can't remember," I said.

Father Sanon looked at Delta, then Ma calmed herself down some and said in Creole, "Dee Dee, go look after the babies."

Delta walked out of the kitchen, but I didn't hear her go up the stairs.

Then Ma said, "Tell them what happened, Karina."

So I told Father Sanon what Ma had told me had happened the night that Enid was attacked and she was hauling boxes at the bottling factory.

Mr. Levinson said that we shouldn't worry, he knew just who to speak with. Father Sanon then explained that Mr. Levinson ran a community center that helped new immigrants with whatever they needed.

"There are so many Haitian families going through the same problems that you are," said Mr. Levinson. "There have been a few cases of abuse of Haitian children that were pretty bad, and I think the authorities may be quicker to judge everyday situations in families like yours—discipline, sibling rivalry—as abuse."

He was talking to Ma but mostly looking at Father Sanon, as if expecting him to translate. Father Sanon just nodded and said nothing. Ma sniffed a lot. "Don't worry, Mrs. Gaston," said Mr. Levinson as he reached over and patted her arm. "We will do everything we can to get your family back together."

I could not believe what I was hearing. Yeah, I knew what I had just told Father Sanon and Mr. Levinson. But if they couldn't tell I was lying, then they were major-league retards. Why did I keep thinking some adult somewhere was finally going to start acting like one? Why did I think that Aunt Merlude would know what else to do when she found Enid half dead besides collapsing into a babbling heap of drool? Why did I think Uncle Jude would drive us all to the police station and rat out his brother instead of dunking Enid in a scalding salt bath, then letting the Daddy crash at his apartment? Why did I think that Mr. Levinson would listen to me tell him how I'd beaten Enid so badly she was still limping this many weeks later, then nod his head and pat my arm and say, "Bullshit, Karina"?

Father Sanon and Ma stood up and closed their eyes and held their arms out to the ceiling and began to pray. Mr. Levinson stood too and started to walk out of the kitchen. He looked at me and cocked his head toward the hallway. I followed.

"What grade are you in, Karina?" Mr. Levinson smiled at me, but his eyes kept twitching back to the kitchen, where Ma and Father Sanon were really getting into it. Father Sanon kept praying louder and louder to be heard over Ma's crying.

Mr. Levinson's breath smelled like knishes and old cheese. I took two steps away from him and crossed my arms over my chest. "I'm going into eighth," I said.

"Ah, last year of middle school. That should be fun."

"Yeah, right," I whispered.

"I have a daughter about your age. She just graduated from middle school." Then he got quiet, as if expecting me to say something. I shrugged, then turned and headed for the stairs. Ma and Father Sanon came out of the kitchen just then, and Mr. Levinson said, "Mrs. Gaston, I was thinking that if it is okay with you, maybe Karina could visit us at the community center, maybe even volunteer a couple of days a week."

I spun around on the steps and almost fell. Ma was wiping tears from her face.

"If that's okay with you, Karina," said Mr. Levinson.

I shook my head, then opened my mouth, but nothing came out.

"I think that is a very good idea," said Father Sanon.

"Yes, yes," said Ma.

"We love having young people of all different backgrounds talk to new immigrants about life in America. You can even help them read their mail or talk to utility companies on their behalf," said Mr. Levinson. "Or if you'd like, you can help tutor some of the younger kids in English. What do you think about that?"

"She very smart," said Ma.

"Have you given any thought to what you'd like to be when you grow up, Karina?"

I shrugged, and Ma said, "She want to be book writer. She always telling stories."

"Excellent, excellent," said Mr. Levinson. "How does this Monday sound? Can I count on you for Monday?"

I wanted to say that I really didn't care to be helping out the guy who was about to do whatever he could with the authorities to get the Daddy back home, but what I said was, "I don't know where the center is."

Ma said, "Uncle Jude take you." Then she turned to Mr. Levinson and said, "She come Monday."

I ran up the stairs.

Up in our bedroom Delta was waiting for me. "You lied to a priest, Katu," she said. "That's a sin."

"So why don't you go downstairs and tell him what really happened?" I asked, sitting down on our bed. "You can't and you know it because you know Father

Sanon *wanted* to be lied to and you know Ma *wanted* me to lie to him."

"It's still a sin! And you don't know what Father Sanon wants. You can't read his mind!"

I jumped off our bed and opened the bedroom door. "Go tell him the truth, then, Delta!"

Delta didn't move. I walked over to her, grabbed her by the shirt, and dragged her to the door. "I said go tell him the truth!"

She stood in the doorway, crying and looking at me. Miss Smarty-pants, little Miss Perfect, too close to God to be expected to lie, so Ma makes me do it. I swung both arms out at her chest and shoved her hard. She skidded on her back to the top of the stairs. I slammed the door closed and turned the lock.

Delta never did go tell Father Sanon the truth that day. Later in the afternoon Ma sent us to clean Uncle Jude's apartment, and I apologized for shoving her by letting Delta choose the radio stations and records we listened to while we cleaned. She accepted my apology by picking my favorite stations and playing Prince on the record player over and over.

An awful lot of people kept coming in and out of our house over the next few days. Most were fat ladies from Aunt Merlude's church. But some were people we recognized from Father Sanon's church. They were filing in and out of the house and kissing Ma on the cheek and rubbing her back like someone had died, even though when we were at Father Sanon's Mass, we'd never seen those people talk to Ma at all. We all just stayed up in my bedroom most of the time or ran up there whenever we heard the doorbell ring. Ma didn't ask me to come down and explain again what had happened that night. She did the explaining for me, and once in a while I'd listen from the top of the stairs and learn just how mean I had been to Enid.

Mostly the people who came over whispered and prayed and told Ma not to worry because jails in New York weren't like in Haiti. The Daddy would be fed; she didn't have to bring food to him. They'd give him clothes to wear and a place to take a shower, and they'd give him a lawyer to talk to for free. Father Sanon would go with her to visit him. He'd even bring him Communion—just the body, though, not the blood.

My birthday is usually easy to remember because it's the day before the Fourth of July. Everyone's getting ready to go to a barbecue or invite people to their own barbecue or figure out where to sit in the park to watch the fireworks. Ma used to say that the only thing the Fourth of July made her think about was when I was born and she was holding me and seeing fireworks for the first time in her life from the window of her hospital room. She said all those colors exploding in the sky was just like what she was feeling inside.

I always get a present on my birthday and everyone sings "Happy Birthday" to me, but most years Ma saves the cake and the balloons until just before the fireworks the next night. It's like having two birthdays back-to-back, and it's a good thing, too, 'cause the year the Daddy died I didn't have a birthday at all. Ma didn't exactly forget. She just wasn't in a celebrating mood.

On Fourth of July night Delta and the twins and Gerald and Roland and I took blankets out to the porch and lay on our backs to watch the fireworks. We could only see the really big ones, since the park was far away and surrounded by great big trees. Enid came out for a little while and so did Augustin. Aunt Merlude and Gran watched from inside the kitchen, worried sick that the sparks would land on the deck and set us all on fire.

Halfway through the show Delta rolled over on her side and finally said what had been on her mind: "I don't understand why you would call the cops, Katu, and then not tell the truth."

I rolled over on my side so I could face her. "I didn't call them, Dee Dee, honest. Actually, I thought you did."

Delta shook her head, and we both looked up at Enid.

"Why would I do something so stupid?" said Enid. "Like it would ever help?"

"Then, who . . . ?" I started to ask, but just then Delta shouted, "Oh, yeah! Happy birthday yesterday, Katu!"

10.

The following Monday, Uncle Jude picked me up and took me to the community center. I thought he'd come in with me, but he didn't.

"Call when you finish," he said, and then drove off.

I stood outside the door to the community center for a while, trying to figure out if there was someplace else I could hide out for a couple hours before calling Uncle Jude to come pick me up. The community center was smack in the middle of a row of stores, squished between a Laundromat and a pizza place. On the other side of the Laundromat was a used bookstore. I looked in through the window, and mostly what they had in there was comic books. I hate comic books.

I went back to the front of the pizza store and looked in again. I didn't have any money for pizza, just eighty-eight cents, enough change to play three games of Centipede or three games of Pac-Man and make a phone call. I liked Centipede more, but I was way better at Pac-Man, so it would take a lot longer to lose. I figured if I was lucky, I could kill almost an hour in there. Okay, maybe thirty minutes. I'd made up my mind to go in when I saw a familiar red reflection in the pizza store window and turned around.

Across the parking lot was another row of stores, only not as long as the row with the pizza store and the community center. On one corner was a bank. Next to that was a Chinese restaurant, then a store with wooden boards on the window, and next to that was a liquor store. Uncle Jude's taxi was parked in front of the liquor store. I was getting really annoyed with Uncle Jude and wondered if he'd ever calm down with all the drinking. I mean, I liked him a whole lot more than the Daddy, but I was beginning to think that if the Daddy didn't beat us to death first, Uncle Jude would one day fall asleep at the wheel of his taxi and turn us all into roadkill.

No way could I hide out now and call Uncle Jude to pick me up. I'd have to make up a story and get Mr. Levinson to take me back home. I decided to skip Pac-Man and go into the stupid community center and get it over with.

There were bells hanging over the door, and when I entered, they made a racket and everyone looked up at me and smiled like they had been awaiting my arrival all day long. There were three desks in that front room, one against each wall except the wall with the front door. At each desk sat a white lady, and beside each of them were some black and Chinese people. The white lady at the desk to my right came over to me and said, "You must be Ka-*rrr*-ina! William told us you might be helping us out today! Welcome!"

"Um, same to you . . . I mean, thank you." This was going to be way more annoying than I thought.

"My name is Laurel, and this is Patty and that's Bethel!" Laurel pointed to the white ladies sitting at each desk. She didn't say who the black and Chinese people with them were.

"Let's see, where should we start?!"

Bethel said, "Why don't you get Rachael to give her a tour?"

"That's a wonderful idea! Would you like a tour of our little community center?!"

Jeez, anything to get away from you. "That sounds so cool!" I yelled. Then I grinned so wide my lips cracked, and I hunched my shoulders up like Laurel and swayed from side to side. I wanted to hop up and down, too, but figured that might be taking it a tad too far.

"Well, let's go, then!" she said as she put her arm around my shoulders and led me to a door next to Bethel's desk. Totally clueless.

We went through a long hallway with doors up and down either side. Laurel stopped at the last door on the right and knocked. She didn't wait for an answer before opening it. The room looked like a day-care center, with the walls covered in kids' crayon drawings. Against the back wall a row of milk crates were stacked five or six high with the open sides facing out. The crates were jammed with toys and coloring books and crayons and Dr. Seuss and Curious George books. There was a playpen on one side of the room but no baby in it. In the middle of the room were tiny tables with tiny chairs around them. Two little boys sat scribbling on Tom and Jerry pictures torn from a coloring book.

On the other side of the room was a regular-size desk like the ones we have at school. A white girl about my age was sitting there cutting pictures out of a magazine. She had long brown hair, thick and straight except in the front, where she'd curled and poofed it up real big and hair-sprayed it stiff. She hadn't looked up when we came in, but I could tell by her hair and the clothes she had on that she was probably real pretty.

Laurel said, "Rachael? We have a new volunteer today! Ka-*rrr*-ina, this is Rachael! Rachael, Ka-*rrr*-ina!"

The girl still didn't look up. Laurel said, "Would you mind giving her a tour of the center, please?"

Rachael finally looked over at us and said, "Can't you see I'm busy?"

I was wrong about her being pretty. She was totally gorgeous, and I could see that even though she was all covered in goofy-colored makeup. Her nose was pudgy and round. She had deep dimples that showed in her cheeks even though she wasn't smiling. Her eyebrows were so thick I bet I could have braided them. But what made her really beautiful were her eyes. I couldn't tell what color they were, standing there in the doorway, but I could tell they were dark and bright at the same time.

"A tour will only take a few minutes," said Laurel. She'd stopped yelling in that annoying Valley girl voice. I guess yelling for her meant she was happy. What an airhead.

"Besides," continued Laurel, "I'm sure afterward Ka-*rrr*-ina would be happy to help you with the collage. Right, Ka-*rrr*-ina?"

"Sure," I said.

"Okay, Rachael?" Laurel asked in a not-a-question tone.

"Whatever," said Rachael as she went back to cutting out pictures. Laurel squeezed my shoulders, then left the room.

Rachael looked up again and said, "Do you mind?"

"About what?" I asked.

"Duh, the door?"

I closed the door and went over and sat on the floor in front of the milk crates. There were no Encyclopedia Brown books, which were my favorite kid books. I scanned the Curious George books and pulled out the one where George escapes from the man in the big yellow hat and gets all tangled up in spaghetti in some restaurant kitchen. I know those books are for, like, really little kids, but I laugh every time I read the part where George gets high from sniffing a bottle of ether and has to be dunked in cold water after he passes out.

One of the little boys stopped coloring and came over to me.

"Hi," I said.

He just stared, first at me and then at the book in my lap.

"You want to read this one?" I asked as I held out the book to him.

He said nothing.

"He doesn't speak any English," Rachael said from across the room.

"Oh," I said.

"And even if he did, does he *look* like he's old enough to read?"

"Well, what language does he speak?" I asked Rachael. I noticed she had stopped with the collage and was sitting back in her chair, arms folded, watching me.

"Haitian," she answered.

"You mean Creole?" I said.

"Whatever."

"What's your name?" I asked the boy in Creole.

He smiled a tiny bit and said, "Pierre."

"How old are you?"

He used his left hand to hold down his right pinky and thumb, then held up the remaining fingers for me to see. Then he looked down at the Curious George book.

"Is that your brother?" I asked, pointing to the other little boy, who was still at the tiny table but had stopped coloring and was watching us.

Pierre nodded and said, "Audson." Then he let his right pinky out of the grasp of his left hand.

"Okay." I nodded.

I motioned for Audson to come over and sit down next to me. Pierre sat on my other side. I didn't know the Creole word for "curious," so I told Pierre and Audson that the book was about a monkey named George who wants to know everything. Then I flipped through and translated the story for them.

They laughed and laughed, even at parts that

weren't really funny. I figured they were more amused by my Creole than by Curious George flinging himself off a fire escape and breaking his leg. Gran and Aunt Jacqueline always said that my sisters and I had heavy tongues, and they sometimes laughed like Pierre and Audson were laughing whenever we spoke Creole.

Rachael couldn't have known that, though I think I caught her smiling while I read to the boys and they laughed. But she quickly put her angry face back on and hunched over her collage when Laurel came into the room again.

"Oh, Ka-*rrr*-ina, thank you so much for reading to them!" Laurel walked across the room and held out a hand for each boy.

"Time to say bye-bye! Can you say 'bye-bye'?!" Audson and Pierre took hold of Laurel's hands but said nothing.

"How about 'thank . . . you . . . Ka-*rrr*-ina'?!" The boys looked at Laurel like she had horns growing out of her forehead. Laurel led them out of the room. Rachael got up from her desk and slammed the door shut.

"God, she's so annoying," Rachael said to the door, then she turned to me. "What are you laughing about?"

I hadn't realized I was laughing. I guess reading with Pierre and Audson had put me in a good mood even though I didn't want to be in one.

"Nothing," I said. "What time is it?"

"Time to get a watch," she said, then as I headed to the door, she asked, "Where are you going?"

I shrugged. "Wanna give me the tour?"

"Not really."

I shrugged again and opened the door. "I need to get a ride home," I said.

I didn't care whether or not I got a tour. I figured I'd been at the community center long enough, and translating Curious George for Audson and Pierre was enough good-deed volunteer work for the guy who wanted to nominate the Daddy for the Father of the Year award. I was ready to leave.

"Oh God, wait," said Rachael. "I'll give you the stupid tour. I don't need any more trouble."

"What trouble?" I asked.

Rachael didn't answer. I followed her down the hallway. She stopped at a door, opened it, and pointed in. "This is the meeting room," she said. I'd barely gotten a glance in before she slammed the door shut and moved on to another room.

"This is the storage room for pens, paper, social services forms, and stuff. . . . This is William's office-slash-mock-courtroom. . . . This is the education room for teaching people how to speak English and, like, how not to beat the living shit outta their kids so much. . . . This is the playroom for older kids—don't bother with the board games, there are always more pieces missing than are actually there."

Rachael got to a door she didn't bother to open, only pointed and said, "That's the crapper." I followed her back into the day-care center, where she spun around in the middle of the room with her arms stretched out and said in Laurel's annoying voice, "And this is where we look after the younger children while their parents are in the center learning how to better their lives in their new homeland!"

I laughed. "You totally sound just like her."

Rachael dropped back into her chair and picked up her scissors and a magazine.

"Do you know when Mr. Levinson will be back?" I asked.

Rachael shrugged, then checked her watch. "But he better be back soon. The center closes in a little while, and I don't want to be here a second longer than I have to be."

Just at that moment Mr. Levinson walked into the room.

"Thank God," said Rachael.

"Ready to go, girls?" he asked.

"Yeah," I said. Rachael picked up her purse and headed for the door.

"How would you like to join us for dinner, Karina?" asked Mr. Levinson. "I've spoken to your mom, and she says it's okay. And I'm sure Rachael would like to spend more time with her new friend, right, honey?"

"Dad!" Rachael yelled. "That's so not fair! I'm grounded and can't hang out with my *real* friends, but you can pick out new ones for me?"

Mr. Levinson gave Rachael a look, and she stomped her foot and stormed out of the room.

"I didn't know you were her father," I said.

"Sometimes I think she forgets it too," said Mr. Levinson.

I wasn't thrilled to be having dinner with Mr. Levinson, but to tell you the truth, as mean as Rachael was trying to be to me, I wasn't, like, totally upset to spend more time with her. Rachael and I rode in the backseat while Mr. Levinson drove and babbled on about our great melting pot of a community and how important it was for people of different races and religions and cultures to get to know one another. For a minute there I thought he was going to pull the car over and make us get out and sing "We Are the World" in the middle of the highway.

Rachael was really fuming. She said nothing at all, didn't even answer when her father asked how the collage project was coming along.

"I hope you'll be joining us at the center again, Karina," said Mr. Levinson. "Laurel told me what a great job you did with the little Wilbert brothers today."

"I'm not sure," I said. "I don't think I can always get a ride back and forth from the center."

"Oh?" said Mr. Levinson. "How did you get there today? You didn't hitchhike, I hope." Ha, ha, ha.

"My uncle dropped me off, but he's usually very busy," I said. *Busy getting drunk.*

"I see." Mr. Levinson nodded.

"And today I thought if you didn't show up, I'd have to ask that Laurel lady for a ride home," I said.

"She would have been more than happy to take you, I'm sure."

"Yeah, but I'd rather stick a fork in my eye and twist the handle until my eyeball popped out than spend fifteen minutes stuck in a car with her."

Rachael positively howled. She laughed so hard her eyes started to tear. I smiled too. I was glad Rachael had cheered up. Mr. Levinson wasn't so amused.

"Well, I know Laurel has her own special ways," he said. "But her heart is in the right place."

Mr. Levinson pulled up to a big, fancy house with four white pillars from the roof to the floor of the front porch. The driveway wasn't a regular driveway. It was one of those semicircle things where you drive in at one side and drive out the other. I'd never been in this part of Chestnut Valley before. I never even knew Chestnut Valley had parts like this. Even the Mrs.'s house where Aunt Merlude worked wasn't this fancy.

I followed Rachael into the house; the front door wasn't even locked. Totally not a smart idea for a rich person's house, but maybe they had a guard dog or a butler or something.

"Mom!" Rachael shouted. "We've got a visitor!"

Rachael turned to me then and watched as I looked over her house. We were in a big foyer with a chandelier hanging in the middle. There was a living room on the right side with a big white piano, and even though the furniture was the fanciest I'd ever seen, fancier than even the living rooms of white people that I'd seen on TV, they hadn't bothered to cover it with plastic. The room on the left of the foyer was the dining room. There was another chandelier hanging in there over a really,

really long, shiny wooden table that was already set for dinner.

Mr. Levinson finally walked in and called, "Honey? Where are you?" Then he disappeared toward the back of the house.

I took a few steps toward the dining room because I wanted to make sure my eyes weren't playing tricks on me. I thought I saw from the foyer that each place setting had, like, three forks and three spoons. I was right. I was trying to figure out why in the world anyone would need so much silverware to eat a meal when suddenly I heard, "Ka-*rrr*-ina! We're so happy you could join us for dinner!"

I turned around and Laurel practically jumped me with a bear hug. Rachael started that howling laugh again, then she disappeared up the stairs.

"Dinner will be ready in half an hour, Ka-*rrr*-ina," said Laurel. "Why don't you join Rachael up in her room."

11.

Ray, Roy, Robby. Robby, Ray, Roy. Every darn inch of Rachael's bedroom walls was covered with posters of the guys from Menudo. Rachael lay on her bed flipping through a magazine. The magazine was full of posters of singers and bands and television stars. I looked around the room and wondered if she was planning on taking down some Menudo posters to make space for those new ones, or if she'd just start plastering the ceiling.

"Why didn't you tell me Laurel was your mom?"

Rachael shrugged.

"If I ever spoke to my mom the way you spoke to your mother at the center . . . well, let's just say I'd never speak to my mom that way," I said.

"Why do people from your country like to smack kids around so much?" she asked.

"I'm from America, so I wouldn't know," I said. "Besides, if kids act the way you do to grown-ups, they deserve to be smacked around."

"Boy, you'll be a great mother someday," she said. "Right after a judge sentences you to one of my dad's classes."

"Your dad should be sentenced to his own class."

"Sorry to break it to you, but we're civilized people. My parents never hit us."

"Of course not, when would they have time? They're too busy getting other parents outta jail so they can go home and hit their own kids," I said. "Maybe I'll get a job like that when I grow up, then I can afford a mansion like this."

Rachael's room was bigger than the one I shared with Enid and Delta and Gerald. Instead of a regular twin bed for one person, she had one as big as the one in Ma's room. The floor was covered by a fuzzy pink carpet, and all her furniture was white with gold-colored decorations and gold handles on the dresser drawers. The room was real neat. I hadn't spotted a butler yet, but I was sure she didn't clean it herself.

"But I thought your dad didn't really hit you guys," she said. "My dad said that it was a misunderstanding."

"He's not my real father," I said.

There was a television and record player in one corner of her bedroom. I walked over and flipped on the TV. There was nothing good on. I turned it off.

"Anyway, you're just as dumb as your dad if you believe all those people at the center got there 'cause of some great big misunderstanding," I said.

Rachael was quiet, looking at me like she was searching her brain for the perfect comeback. But all she said finally was, "Don't cry."

"I'm not crying, stupid," I said as I tried a doorknob to what I thought was a closet. It wasn't.

"You have your own bathroom," I said.

"Thanks for the bulletin."

I turned back to her television and started fiddling with the dials again.

"What's your favorite show?" I asked.

"I dunno."

"Mine's *The A-Team*. Who's your favorite band?"

"Duh," she said, looking around her bedroom walls.

"Oh, right. I like Prince. Why are you grounded?"

"None of your beeswax."

"How long you grounded for?"

"Till August."

I pointed to one of the Menudo posters and asked, "Do you even understand any of their songs?"

"Who cares what they're saying?" she answered. "They're totally hot!"

I took a hairbrush from her dresser and walked over to the bed. "Know what I think?"

"No idea," she said, eyeing the brush nervously.

"You'd be even prettier if you didn't poof the front of your hair up so big," I said as I handed her the hairbrush. "Try brushing out the hair spray."

Rachael grabbed the brush from me and sat up. She laughed and pointed at my head. "You've got your hair braided into a Mohawk, and you're giving *me* hairstyling advice?"

I flopped onto her bed, resting my head in my palm and my elbow on a pillow. "Plus, you don't need so much blush, and all that blue around your eyes makes you look like Boy George," I said.

Rachael jumped up from the bed and went to stand

in front of her mirror. "I do not look like Boy George," she said as she pulled out a tissue and began blotting her makeup.

"Boy George isn't so bad looking," I said.

"Boy George is a freak," said Rachael.

"Right, a not-so-bad-looking freak," I said. "Kinda like you."

Rachael turned to me. "What the hell is your problem?"

"I don't have a problem," I said as nicely as I could. "I just don't think you need to wear so much makeup."

Rachael went back to blotting her face.

"So why won't you tell me why you're grounded?" I asked.

"Smoking," she said.

"You like cigarettes?"

"I wasn't smoking cigarettes," she answered.

"No way! You're on drugs?"

Rachael sure didn't look like the drug addicts in the health class films they showed in school. All skinny and pale and pimply and greasy haired. Half my school looked like that, but not Rachael. Once a drug counselor, or cop or whatever he was, came and gave a presentation to the whole school. He told all these horrible stories about kids getting hooked on drugs and ending up dead in the street or choking on their own vomit while they slept. But the grossest story he told was about this girl who did so much drugs that she had no cartilage inside her nose. He told us that he'd watched as she put a handkerchief up one nostril and pulled it out of the other. I tried to look up Rachael's pudgy nose, but I couldn't tell if she had all of what was supposed to be up there or if it was just a big, empty space.

"I don't do drugs," said Rachael. "I just smoked a couple of joints."

"What was it like?" I asked.

"Wanna try?" said Rachael with a huge smile on her face.

"No!" I said as I looked around her room, trying to figure out where she had her stash. "I was just wondering."

"Well, I was just kidding," she said. "I don't have any left. No need to freak out."

"I got drunk once," I said.

"So whaddaya want, a medal?"

"Is smoking pot like getting drunk?"

"I don't know. I can't explain it." Rachael seemed bored all of a sudden. Then she got all serious on me.

"Why don't you go live with your real father if your stepdad is mean to you?"

Just remembering what Enid had said made me feel light headed. In a flash I saw myself spilling my guts to Rachael about why I was born and how I didn't even know who my real father was, and I saw me hugging her and touching her hair. But really it was none of her business, I decided. Besides, I'd known her for barely a few hours. It was way too soon to let her know how freaky my life was. I took a deep breath, then bit down on my lower lip. That keeps me from fainting sometimes.

Rachael got off her bed and came toward me. "Are you okay?" Rachael asked. "You look funny."

"I think your mom is calling us for dinner," I said as I walked past her and out of the bedroom.

12.

Before the Daddy left, Sunday mornings were the calmest times at home. We would wake up to the smell of breakfast and dinner cooking at the same time. Ma liked to have dinner all done by the time we went to church so that she'd be able to rest on at least part of the Lord's day before going to work at night.

Sunday dinners were nothing like we had during the week. Instead of boiling the plantains, Ma would slice the sweetest ones she could find, soak them in salt water, then deep-fry them. Instead of baked chicken, we might have *griot*, bite-size chunks of pork hock seasoned to almost too salty, fried until crisp and drizzled with homemade *peekles* so hot and spicy, it made our foreheads sweat. The red beans and rice she'd cook with extra coconut milk, and chop lettuce and tomatoes and hot peppers into it.

But it was the smell of Sunday breakfast that made us wake with our mouths watering. Dried, salty cod bits fried with eggs and big chunks of onions and red peppers, all served with sweet boiled plantains. If Ma was in a good mood, she'd even let us have a tiny bit of Haitian coffee in a cup of sugared milk. We never drank it straight from the cup. We'd dip as much buttered white bread into the mix as it took to finish it.

And on Sunday mornings Haitian music ruled the house. No country music or talk radio, which was about all we could get on the AM clock radio perched on the shelf above the kitchen sink. Ma would leave open the baby gate that was set up in front of the living room to keep us all off the good furniture and out of the record collection and away from the color television, and put on Tabou Combo or Coupé Cloué as loud as she pleased.

Eventually we'd get out of bed and sneak down-stairs and watch from the hallway as Ma shuffled her feet back and forth in front of the stove, swinging her arms in a slow-motion double-Dutch twirl to keep time to the bass. When she spotted us watching her, smiling and giggling and mimicking her pop-the-hip-drop-the-knees-twirl-the-jump-ropes move, she'd stop dancing and remind us she wouldn't stand for being late to church. That was our invitation to sit down to Sunday breakfast.

But for many Sundays after Enid's beat-up I didn't wake with my mouth watering. I didn't smell *griot* baking or plantains frying. There was no music play-ing. The house was still except for the sound of muffled crying that sometimes came from downstairs.

I imagined sometimes that the crying was Ma upset at the Daddy for treating her kids so miserably. Then I imagined sometimes that she was crying just because she had kids. I imagined sometimes that the crying was Enid when her cuts opened up again. Sometimes I imagined the crying was Aunt Merlude. That was easiest, since Aunt Merlude had done an awful lot of praying and crying even before Enid's beat-up.

And Gran. She was the only one who didn't work and could come and stay with us and look after Enid. That's why they'd brought her up from the city. I didn't want to imagine her crying because we didn't have any spare aunts or moms or grandmas to do the job. And they certainly weren't going to leave me, the fainting queen, in charge of anything.

The Sunday morning after the week I first met Rachael, I rolled over in bed to look out the window, trying to stay quiet and not wake the others, and suddenly realized that everyone else in the room was awake. Delta lay in Enid's bed with her arms crossed under her head, staring at the ceiling. Gerald lay beside her, rocking himself slowly and staring at the door. The twins were in my bed, lying head to toe, their eyes darting from everything and every person in the bedroom. When Aunt Merlude came to get them ready for Pentecostal church, I closed my eyes and pretended to be asleep. I think Gerald and Delta did too.

I eventually fell asleep listening to the crying, assuming we'd be skipping Sunday Mass that day like we had for several weeks in a row. But Ma woke us just a little while before church was supposed to start and told us to get dressed. She didn't say anything about bathing, so none of us bothered. She didn't say anything about breakfast, either, but she stuck a bottle in Roland's mouth on our way out of the house.

Saint Anne's Church was only a few blocks away, but we never walked because of the high-heeled shoes Ma wore. Now that the Daddy wasn't around and we had no car to take us to church, we didn't have a choice. Ma wore her heels anyway. We didn't put Gerald's braces on, but after the first block it was obvious he'd never make it all the way to church on his own messed-up legs. I handed Roland to Delta and carried Gerald the rest of the way. By the time I arrived, a half block behind everyone else, my arms were numb and I was sweating like a pig.

Mass hadn't begun yet, but I spotted Ma toward the front, bent over a pew with her forehead against her clasped hands. I started to bring Gerald to her, then noticed that Delta was waving frantically at me from one of the middle pews.

"Ma says to keep the babies with us when we go to English service," Delta whispered as I slipped in next to her.

"We don't have to come back here first?" I asked.

Delta shook her head. "Ma says she has an appointment." Delta made the sign of the cross and bowed to the giant Jesus hanging on the cross as the processional passed our row. "She said to walk home after English church."

Delta, Enid, and I always stayed at the Haitian Mass for only about twenty minutes, up to the part where the priest's helper guy held up the Bible and showed it to the congregation, first to one side, then the middle, then to the other side, like a kindergarten teacher stopping

to show her kids the pictures from the book she is reading to them. I guess they do that to prove to everyone
that it really is the Bible they're reading from up there.

At that point we would leave the gym and go to the
actual chapel, where the English service was held. Ma
had been letting us do that for only about two years. Up
until then we all had attended the Haitian Mass from
beginning to end. The only problem was we had had
absolutely no idea what was going on.

See, even though Haitians speak Creole most of the
time, they switch to regular French for important stuff
like church or weddings or meetings with important
people or when they don't want us kids to know what
they're saying. Creole is close enough to French so
that when Ma or the Daddy spoke kinda slow, I could
figure out most of what they were saying. But Father
Sanon mumbled, and he mumbled quickly. We had
been begging Ma to let us go to English Mass for the
longest time, not because any one of us was particu-
larly interested in what was going on, but because the
English service lasted fifty minutes and the Haitian one
went on for almost two hours. I once asked Ma if I could
skip church altogether, since I didn't believe in God,
but she slapped me and made me take it back.

Ma's compromise was that we had to go to Haitian
Mass until the English one started, then we'd go over
there and afterward come back for the end of Haitian
Mass. I figured at least that would let us break up the
day and we wouldn't be so bored. But once I actually
heard and understood what the priest was saying when

he held up the Communion cup and the Communion wafers and all the other stuff going on, I wished we had stayed at Haitian Mass. At least there I could daydream about whatever I wanted to daydream about without listening to how Jesus had died 'cause of something I did that I needed to be sorry for forever, or hearing stories about drinking blood and eating body parts.

The weird thing is, though, going to the English service had the exact opposite effect on Delta than it did on me and Enid. Delta got *really* into it. She stood up every time we were supposed to; she kneeled on the footrest and closed her eyes and clasped her hands to her face when everybody else did; and she made the sign of the cross constantly. She even woke up early on Tuesdays, Wednesdays, and Fridays during the summer to go to weekday-morning Mass. And unlike with school, Delta was never late for church. She pretty much became Ma's favorite daughter once she started doing that. Enid and I didn't even consider competing with her. Church on weekdays in the summertime when no one was making you go? As if!

Enid and I made fun of Delta at first. But when she was kneeling in prayer after taking Communion one Sunday, and I leaned over and asked her if she thought the body of Christ she had in her mouth was a breast or leg piece, she started to choke. I pounded on her back until she coughed up the wafer. Delta caught it in her hand and stuffed it back into her mouth.

She looked at me all weepy and real serious and said, "Katu, you just have to *believe*. If you *really* believe, God will know we're trying to be good, and then we can be saved."

She said it loud enough that people around us were staring at me like I was the devil's spawn. It was embarrassing, but I felt even worse for Dee Dee. I didn't know how to tell her the only way we'd be saved was if that giant iron Jesus himself came down off the cross and whacked the Daddy upside the head.

Even though Enid and I were real pissed that the three of us ended up going to Sunday school for a whole semester to get ready for our first Communion because Delta had asked Ma to enroll us, we stopped picking on her and left Delta alone with her God thing after that day. Enid just tried not to fall asleep in church. I tried not to scratch too much.

I didn't expect the service to be exactly like the Haitian service the first time we went. But it was, pretty much. There were only three differences. First, of course, they spoke English. Second, Father Carl's sermon was only a few minutes long. We finally figured out that's what made Haitian Mass so long. Father Sanon's sermon alone was as long as the entire English-speaking service. And the third difference was in dress. Haitian people dress like they're going to a wedding every single Sunday. Ma says it's to show God some respect. The Daddy said people dressed up when they went to court to see a judge or when they went to work to see their bosses, and none of them were as important as God. The Daddy wore the same tent pants every Sunday for church, but he always had a different clean white shirt and switched between his two ties.

The people at the English service dressed like . . . well, they dressed for whatever it was they'd be doing *after* church. In the summertime even some of the grown-ups wore shorts and T-shirts. Ma says that shows white people have no respect for God. Even black Americans dress up to go to church, she says.

Delta always took an aisle seat in the chapel so that she could shake Father Carl's hand when it was time to offer one another the sign of the peace. And that first Sunday we went back to church, she had an even better reason to be there. She had been chosen to do one of the readings. I was surprised; she didn't look nervous at all. She sat with one arm around Gerald, her head bent and her eyes closed, looking all holy like she did every Sunday. I sat on the other side of Gerald, and on my other side was Roland. I put Delta's purse in Roland's lap so he'd have something to play with when he finished his bottle.

When Delta got up to go do her reading, I had to hold Gerald to keep him from following her down the aisle. Delta climbed the steps to the altar and pulled a stool from beneath the podium and stood on it. You could still just barely see her head.

She read in a real loud and mature voice. After she finished she bowed her head in silence for a moment.

Gerald was even more proud of Delta than I was, 'cause as she lifted her head and stepped off the stool, he began to clap and yell, "Yeah, Dee Dee!" Then

Roland's bottle fell to the floor when he opened his mouth to squeal and clap his hands. A few people started to laugh. I could see Delta was mortified but I couldn't help it; I laughed too.

I'd taken Communion only a couple times before, but that Sunday morning I was starving, and it looked like the Communion wafer would be the closest thing to food I got for a while. I carried Roland, and Delta held Gerald's hand as we made our way toward Father Carl. Father Carl smiled when he saw me. "The body of Christ," he said as he held the wafer up in front of my face.

"Amen," I said, then he popped it into my mouth. Wet cardboard. That's what the body of Christ tastes like. Father Carl used his thumb to make the sign of the cross on Roland's forehead, then patted him on the head. He did the same to Gerald after Delta received Communion. Gerald loved it. Father Sanon never rubbed any kids' heads at Haitian Mass.

Our old Sunday-school teacher Christopher was doing the communal wine. He didn't look as happy to see me as Father Carl had. Christopher and I haven't gotten along ever since that day in Sunday school when I explained to some of the younger kids what a virgin was and why the mother of Jesus couldn't possibly have been one. When it was my turn, Christopher handed me the cup and said, "The blood of Christ."

"Amen," I said, and took as big a gulp as I could. I was halfway through gulp number two when Christopher grabbed the cup from me, causing some of the wine to splash onto Roland.

I walked quickly back to the pews, and the weirdest thing happened. I all of a sudden wanted to pray for Enid. I didn't know who I should pray to, since I didn't believe in God, so I just closed my eyes real quick and hoped that she wouldn't be in pain for too much longer. I didn't kneel on the footrest and I didn't cross myself afterward, so I don't even know if it really counted.

Right after that was when I decided I couldn't put up with my panty hose any longer. I kicked my shoes off and then, after taking a look around, reached up into my dress real quick and pulled my panty hose down. My underwear almost came too. Gerald started laughing, and I shushed him. I wiggled and wiggled until they were off completely, then stuffed them into Delta's purse. I was bent over buckling my shoes back on when I heard a little voice say, "Eeewww!"

I sat up and saw that Roland had taken my panty hose and flung them onto the pew behind us. He was still holding one end of the panty hose; the rest was on top of a little boy's head. I grabbed them before the little boy's parents came back from the Communion line. Delta looked up and made a face at me.

I leaned over to her and said, "Let's leave now."

She shook her head.

I said, "Communion is the important part, and we did that. Let's *go*."

She shook her head again, and I grabbed her ear and twisted it.

"Owww, Katu!"

Delta has this thing about acting all grown-up just

because she's smarter than me. Smart or not, though, sometimes I have to give her a little reminder of who's older. There really was no reason for us to stay at the service any longer. There really wasn't any reason we'd had to come to service at all, since Ma had said for us to walk home without her. We could have taken the dollars she gave us for the collection plate and hung out at the kosher deli eating knishes. If Delta had been the one beaten too badly to go to church, that's what Enid and I would have done for sure.

Delta moaned and groaned all the way back home. I would have twisted her ear again, but I couldn't be bothered. The sun was really beating down on us, and the blood of Jesus Christ had given me such a wicked buzz I could hardly keep my eyes open. I went to bed as soon as we got home and had to hear from Delta what had happened that afternoon when Ma came home from church with Father Sanon.

13.

"You should have seen it, Katu!" said Delta as she shook my shoulders. "Are you awake?"

"No, I'm not," I said.

I didn't feel as bad as that time Delta and I got drunk off a bottle of wine at Uncle Jude's, but I felt bad enough. My head hurt a little, but mostly it was my stomach. I was hungry and nauseous at the same time.

"Fee Fee cursed out Father Sanon!"

That got my attention. Skipping out on church when you knew you wouldn't be caught was one thing. Not taking Communion when you were in church was not so great either. But cursing out a priest?

"What happened?" I asked as I sat up slowly.

"Didn't you hear all the screaming?"

"Duh," I said. "Would I be asking what happened if I heard it?"

"Father Sanon brought Ma home from church, and he came to give Communion to Fee Fee and Gran, but Fee Fee wouldn't take it," said Delta.

"And?"

"And then Fee Fee said 'hell,' and she said the *f* word."

The school district sure hadn't skipped Delta a grade because of her storytelling skills. She may have an in with the big guy upstairs, if there is one, but it was obvious all the talent for telling a good story that He had given out to this family got split between me and Ma.

"Okay, Dee Dee," I said. "First, what did Father Sanon do when he got here?"

"He went into Aunt Merlude's room to give Communion to Gran and Fee Fee."

"And Fee Fee just said no right away?" I asked.

"No, first he started reading something, then he stopped so that Gran and Fee Fee could say 'Lord hear our prayer,' but they didn't because Father Sanon was doing it in French and they didn't know what he was saying. So then when nobody answered when they were supposed to, he started over in Creole."

"How come Gran didn't answer?"

"Because she doesn't speak French, Katu."

"Oh yeah."

I had almost forgotten. Gran had been visiting with us for a few weeks around the time we were really getting on Ma's case to let us go to the English service. Gran said that when she was a little girl, Mass was said in Latin. Then when she was an adult, the pope said that it was okay to do Mass in whatever language people spoke in their country, so the church she went to switched to French. But Gran didn't understand French, because when she was little, no one bothered sending girls to school. And then when Gran came to the United States, she sometimes would go to English-speaking Mass with Aunt Jacqueline's kids. So Gran said that she didn't know what we all were complaining about, since she hadn't understood Catholic services in three different languages, but that hadn't stopped her from going to church every Sunday and loving Jesus and loving God.

"So did Gran and Fee Fee answer him when he switched over to Creole?" I asked.

"Gran did, but Fee Fee didn't. She just sat there on the bed."

"Then what?"

"Then Father Sanon got to the Communion part, and Gran said, 'Amen,' and took it and made the sign of the cross. But when Father Sanon turned to Fee Fee and said, 'The body of Christ,' Fee Fee wouldn't say 'Amen' and she wouldn't open her mouth."

"Where was Ma?" I asked.

"Standing with me in the hallway."

"What did Ma do when Fee Fee wouldn't take Communion, Dee Dee?"

"Well, see, first Father Sanon said to Fee Fee that accepting the body of Christ means your sins have been forgiven, and then Fee Fee said that she hadn't committed any sin, and then that's when Ma freaked out and yelled at Fee Fee and said how could she disrespect God and Father Sanon like that, and that's when she cursed."

"She, like, just yelled 'hell' and 'fuck'?"

"No, Katu," Delta said. Delta actually had the nerve

to be frustrated with me. Like she was giving me all the information I needed to figure out what in the world had gone on that afternoon. I crossed my arms and said nothing. "When Ma said that Fee Fee didn't have any respect for God and Father Sanon, Fee Fee said, 'Where the hell is God's respect for me? Where the hell is Father Sanon's respect for me?' That's what she yelled. Then Ma stepped into the room and slapped Fee Fee in the face and started screaming that God created her and that Daddy worked hard to feed her and that she had no understanding of how hard it is and how expensive it is to raise a family in this country. Then Father Sanon had to hold Ma back from slapping Fee Fee again."

"'Cause that's when Fee Fee said 'fuck'?" I asked.

Delta nodded and said, "Plus something even worse."

Now it was my turn to be frustrated, but I didn't show it because at that point Delta stopped talking and stared at the floor, and I thought she was going to cry. I let her get a hold of herself until she was ready to explain.

When Delta was ready, she whispered, "Fee Fee said that Ma wouldn't have had to marry a fat, black-as-dirt fuck like Gaston if she hadn't kept getting pregnant by married men who already had too many kids to take care of."

"Oh. My. God!"

"Then Ma slapped her again."

"But I thought Father Sanon was holding Ma back."

"Well, he kinda let her go after Fee Fee said that last part."

"I wonder why Fee Fee decided not to take Communion," I said. "I mean, she could have just done it, and Father Sanon would've been outta there in no time."

"Maybe it was because of the prayer Father Sanon said," answered Delta.

"What prayer?"

"During the reading there's that part where the priest names the sick and suffering people he wants Jesus to pay special attention to?"

Delta could tell I had no clue what she was talking about.

"Don't you ever pay attention in church, Katu?"

"Finish the damn story, Delta."

"Well, when a priest says, 'We pray for the sick and the suffering, especially' this person and that person, then that's when you're supposed to say, 'Lord, hear our prayer.'"

"So Fee Fee was mad because Father Sanon prayed for her?" I asked.

"Father Sanon didn't mention Enid in the prayer," said Delta.

"You've got to be totally fuckin' kidding me," I said, because Delta had finally gotten to a part of the story where I could figure out what happened without her spelling it out for me.

"He wanted Fee Fee to say 'Lord, hear our prayer' for brother Gaston."

By the time Delta finished that last sentence, I had already run out of the bedroom and down the stairs, and hurled myself down the last five steps, almost landing on the floor face-first.

"Where is she?" I asked Delta as she came down the stairs and met me coming out of Aunt Merlude's bedroom.

"Outside," she said, pointing toward the kitchen.

Out on the back porch I found Enid on her knees with her arms crossed tightly at her chest, her face as close to the house as it could be without touching it. Her back was straight and stiff, but her shoulders shook as she cried quietly.

I couldn't believe my eyes. I couldn't believe Ma was actually punishing Enid this way.

I turned to Delta and mouthed, "How long?"

Delta leaned toward me and whispered, "Like, an hour."

If Enid had been on her knees for an hour already, based on Ma's usual routine, she might be on her knees for another half an hour or so. When Ma planned on giving us a beat-up, she kept us on our knees for only twenty or thirty minutes. That she intended on beating Enid so soon after the Daddy had given her the worst beat-up anyone ever had didn't even enter my mind.

The Daddy had long ago given up on the ritual of placing us on our knees for a while before beating us. I suppose it was a method of torture that was too indirect for him. But Ma still did it. While she had us on our knees, she'd recount for us in excruciating detail every misdeed we'd ever committed, starting with our kicking her in the ribs while we were in her womb. By the time she got to our present-day crimes, we'd be silently begging for a beating.

It wasn't always that way, though. Before we got used to the Daddy's beat-ups—and believe it or not, the first year after he married Ma, he actually never once hit us—the only thing we'd be begging for on our knees was that a visitor would come to the door.

Ever heard the saying "Saved by the bell"? Well, for some reason, whenever Haitian grown-ups visit other Haitians and find kids on their knees, they ask the parents to pardon the kids and the parents actually do. This doesn't happen right away, though. At least not with the adults who used to come by our place.

Like Uncle Jude, for example. Uncle Jude would come by, see us on our knees, and ask what we did to upset our parents so badly. Then we'd make as good a case as we could for ourselves, explaining how it was all a misunderstanding or an accident or whatever. All the while Uncle Jude would try to keep a straight face. Then he'd go about whatever business he'd come to the house for, and on his way out, pretending it was an afterthought, he'd ask Ma to forgive us. Ma would then state her case, which was always short and simple: "They're rotten, rotten kids."

And Uncle Jude would say that all kids were rotten, but that he had our word that we would never again forget our hat at school or forget to put a fresh roll of toilet paper onto the toilet paper holder thingie or spill milk on the floor or fall asleep with the bedroom light on or commit whatever crime against humanity we had committed.

Then Ma would restate her case. "They're rotten, rotten kids."

And Uncle Jude would say, "Please, please, forgive them for me just this one last time." Meanwhile, we'd be there on our knees, watching and waiting, knowing that we always escaped a beat-up when an adult asked that we be pardoned, but also afraid that maybe, just maybe, this would be the time Ma would not cave in.

That time never did come. But then again, people didn't come over to our house much either. Uncle Jude rarely just dropped in for no reason. Ma's friends stopped coming around once they got to know the Daddy. And the Daddy never had any friends that we knew of except for Augustin. We just figured that since Augustin never asked for us to be pardoned, there was some live-in exception to the whole pardoning ritual written down somewhere.

Once we were getting beat on pretty regularly by the Daddy, Ma's beat-ups weren't so unbearable anymore. For starters, she only used belts, and only on our arms or the backs of our legs. She didn't punch us in the stomach or throw the blender or toaster at our head, although there was the occasional slap in the face. Ma also made us count out our licks, like to ten or twenty, so at least we knew the beating would eventually end.

I had long ago given up on anyone walking through the door of our house just at the moment Ma put us on our knees. Delta always had hope, though, and she didn't appreciate it when I'd start knocking my head against the wall or sighing real loudly to piss Ma off and make her cut her speech short and proceed straight to the beat-up. For Delta's sake I didn't do that too often, only when I thought we'd miss a real good TV show while Ma yacked away and the dirt on the floor got buried farther and farther into the skin of our knees.

"Where's Ma?" I whispered to Delta.

"I think she's upstairs."

I went over to Enid and sat next to her. Delta sat on her other side. We had nothing to say, and for a while the only sounds outside were Enid crying and Delta tapping a piece of wood from the old porch against her shoe. Ma had asked the Daddy over and over to rebuild sections of our porch that were basically rotted out, and he finally did, three years before. But he'd never gotten around to taking the old wood pieces to the junkyard. We'd sometimes use them as baseball bats, but those games were fun only if Enid played nothing but the umpire. Enid was so good at batting that she made the varsity softball team her freshman year, and the coach was always bugging her about joining. The Daddy wouldn't let her play, though, because in his mind the only proper after-school activity for the family's oldest girl was at home watching the rest of us kids.

"How can someone so damn skinny hit so hard?" I'd ask as Enid wailed away on tennis ball after tennis ball, so that we'd have to sneak into backyards three and four houses away to get them back.

"It's all in the *twist*, Katu," she'd say as she

popped her hip like a hula dancer and sent another one flying.

Mostly, though, the slats just sat piled in a corner of the porch, the ones on the outside getting mushier with every rainfall.

Enid was wearing a light cotton robe that barely brushed the porch. From the way her legs were twitching, I could tell she was probably kneeling on pieces of wood that had broken off and were scattered across the porch and on the grass below.

I was about to suggest we get kitchen towels for Enid's knees when Delta gasped and slapped at her mouth. I looked over my shoulder and saw Ma standing in the doorway. She was dressed in sneakers and jeans and a long-sleeved T-shirt, her work clothes. Her hair was pulled back and tied with a silk scarf. She hadn't removed all the makeup she'd worn to church. She had her left hand on her hip and her head cocked. The Daddy's belt dangled from her right hand.

Delta and I jumped up and moved away from Enid. Enid didn't wait to be told to stand up, but it took her a while to get up off her knees. She had to use both hands against the house to steady herself. The whole time she took to stand, she kept her eyes locked on Ma's. Splinters of wood fell from her trembling legs to the porch.

Ma began to wrap the belt around her fist, and then suddenly Enid pulled on one of her straps and let her robe fall to the porch. She stood there in front of Ma, outside in the daytime for all the world to see, completely butt naked. Delta gasped again.

Enid turned to the side and pointed at her left leg and said to Ma in Creole, "I think there's a spot here you can use."

We never speak to Ma in Creole. She speaks Creole, we answer in English. Enid spoke to Ma like she was an adult. We knew then that things would never again be the same between Ma and Enid.

Ma stared back at Enid, eye to eye. She wouldn't look at Enid's naked, bruised, and scarred body, though her eyes kept trying to flick downward.

"I should have left you in Haiti," said Ma. Then she turned and went back inside.

14.

The next morning Ma came into our room early and woke me up. On the bed she placed the outfit I'd worn to church the day before.

"Take a bath and put this on," she said. "We have to go out."

I looked over at Delta, who had slept in our bed instead of on the floor, and then at the twins and Gerald on Enid's bed. They were all still asleep.

"Only you," Ma said before walking out of the room.

I filled the tub with water, but I didn't get in. I was too tired. I sat on the toilet with my head on the sink and wondered where I was going on a Monday morning in my Sunday clothes. Maybe Ma had finally remembered my birthday and was taking me out for a really belated surprise. Not likely.

"Katu, you ready?" Ma yelled from the bottom of the stairs.

From the slobber all over my arms, I figured I'd fallen asleep again. I jumped off the toilet and tried to sound as awake as possible.

"Almost, Ma," I called from behind the closed door.

I let out the water in the tub, splashed water on my face, and then brushed my teeth.

When I got downstairs, Ma and Gran were helping Enid get dressed. She was wearing Sunday clothes too. So was Ma. She even had on a big ole Easter hat. Gran was still in her nightgown and hadn't put her teeth in yet.

"Do they know what to say to the white people?" asked Gran. She licked her lips, then sucked them back into her mouth. She looked like E.T., the extraterrestrial.

"They know," answered Ma. "They know better than me."

I heard noise coming from the kitchen and found Uncle Jude sitting at the table drinking coffee and tearing a piece off a huge roll of bread from the Haitian bakery.

"Good mornin', sweetheart," he said. His eyes weren't red at all. They were the clearest I'd ever remembered seeing them. I kissed him on the cheek and took the piece of bread he held out to me.

"Where are we going?" I whispered.

"Court."

"Why?"

"Daddy maybe come home," he said.

"Maybe?"

Uncle Jude looked toward the hallway, then turned to me and whispered, "You have to tell judge what happened to Fee Fee."

"About the fight I had with Fee Fee, right?"

Uncle Jude looked at me, then looked down at his coffee cup. "You have to tell judge what happened to Fee Fee," he said again, only more slowly this time.

I understood then exactly what Uncle Jude was saying to me. And suddenly I also understood how the police and Clara the social worker had found out about Enid's beat-up. I could hardly believe it.

"Ma said that Daddy is not allowed to give us beat-ups anymore," I said. I couldn't keep the whiny sound out of my voice.

Uncle Jude stood up from the table and said in Creole, "Tell your mother I'm waiting in the car." He left by the back door.

No one spoke on the way to the court. Enid sat with her head leaning against the window and her eyes closed. Ma stared straight ahead. Uncle Jude pulled into the court parking lot and headed for an empty space.

"You can just drop us in the front," said Ma.

"I was going to wait to take you back home," said Uncle Jude.

"I don't think you'll need to," said Ma.

Uncle Jude looked at me through the rearview mirror, then nodded and drove to the front of the courthouse.

I'd never seen the Daddy look the way he did that morning. He looked like he'd lost fifty pounds—all in the face. He walked into the courtroom a few minutes after we did and sat across the room at a table with two men in suits. The white man in a suit whispered something to the black man in a suit, who then leaned over and whispered something into the Daddy's ear.

I looked over to Ma when I heard her grunt and realized that she hadn't grunted, but let out the breath I guess she'd been holding since the Daddy walked in. I looked over to Enid, and she looked like she was about to throw up. I poked her on the leg and she looked at me. I smiled a little, hoping she'd loosen up and not be so scared. She slid a hand over to me. It was shaking. I grabbed it and found it was also wet and cold.

Just then my toes went all wet and cold too. I think it was because of the stupid panty hose, but it may have been the air-conditioning in the courtroom. It was crazy cold in there, but I don't know why Enid would have been so cold. She hadn't worn dress-up clothes since the beat-up, and Gran had been afraid if she wore panty hose, they would get stuck to cuts that hadn't completely healed yet, which would ooze right through the tiny panty hose holes. But Ma had said that she couldn't go bare legged because you could still see scratches and there was a patch just below her left knee that was still a funny blue and green color. So they had put Enid in black panty hose with the only matching black dress she had, which went only to her knees, but the sleeves were long. Enid looked like she was going to a funeral in the middle of the summer. I guess people do die in the summer, but they don't bury them in family court. Anyway, she should have been warm or at least not as cold as me.

Besides the lawyer guys in suits—and there were a

bunch of them—Father Sanon was there and so was Mr. Levinson, who wasn't wearing a suit. He looked nice and everything, but he was wearing tight blue jeans and a white shirt and a brown jacket. He kept looking over to Ma and Enid and me and smiling and nodding. Ma wasn't smiling, her lips were tight and all bunched up, but I thought I saw her nod just a little back at Mr. Levinson. Clara the social worker lady was there too. I tried not to look at her.

When the judge came into the courtroom, everyone stood up except for a lady sitting in front of a tiny typewriter. The judge was fat and bald and looked very tired. He sat down and nodded, then we all sat down.

The judge shuffled some papers around for a while, then looked at the typist and said something about an emergency hearing. I heard him mention the Daddy's name, and I heard him mention Enid's name, but most of the other stuff he said was pretty much gibberish. Then he looked down at his papers again and mumbled a question, and I thought he was just thinking out loud to himself, but then the white man at the Daddy's table stood up.

"Your Honor, as you know, this case has been transferred to family court because of the clear evidence we have that the injuries sustained by the minor in question resulted from a fight with her sister and not from any abuse on the part of her stepfather," he said.

I wondered where the Daddy had gotten the money to hire this guy who dressed like a movie-star lawyer, when half the time he acted like he couldn't spare a buck to get us groceries.

Enid squeezed my hand. The judge said, "Mrs. Wallace?"

Clara stood up and said, "Our office has reason to believe that the story about a fight between the two sisters was told to us because the children are simply too scared to tell the truth."

Clara seemed like she was about to say more, but the judge said, "Ma'am, this case has been removed to family court precisely because the children involved in the alleged incident deny the injuries were caused by the stepfather. However, the report made to children's services alleges ongoing abuse in the home, and we are here today to determine whether that claim has any validity, and if so, what to do about it."

The white man at the Daddy's table stood up again and said, "Your Honor, Mr. Gaston also denies having ever abused his children in any way. However, he is concerned with the effect a prolonged legal case might have on his family and therefore has agreed to complete a course in child rearing. Mr. William Levinson of the We Are One Community Center can speak more on that matter."

That's when Mr. Levinson stood up, but the judge didn't let him speak just yet.

"Yes, yes, I am well acquainted with Mr. Levinson and his position regarding the treatment of immigrant families by the family court," said the judge in kind of a snotty way. "Before I decide whether or not to recommend the class for Mr. Gaston, I'd like to have a chat in my chambers with this young lady. . . ."

The judge shuffled papers some more like he was looking for a name. Everyone looked at Enid, and she looked at me and swallowed hard.

Then the judge said, "Will Karina Lamond step forward, please?"

Clara said, "Your Honor, the minor in question here is Enid Lamond."

The judge said, "And Karina is the sister who supposedly beat her up?"

"Supposedly," said Clara.

"Yes, well, she's the one I'd like to speak to," said the judge. He looked up from his papers finally and said, "Miss Karina Lamond?"

When court ended that day, Ma, Enid, and I got into an elevator to go down to the lobby. Mr. Levinson stuck his hand between the closing doors and got in with us. Nothing bugs me more than when grown-ups laugh at stuff that isn't funny. Or when they start talking about the weather just because they're in the same zip code as another person and they think it'll be rude if they don't say something. I got a double dose of my nightmare in that elevator.

Two floors. That's all it was from the courtroom down to the lobby. But two floors was way too long for Mr. Levinson to keep his trap shut.

So he turned to Ma and said, "Can you believe how hot this summer is?"

And Ma went, "Oh yes, it so hot."

And then they both went, "Heh-heh-heh."

Stuck there with the guy who had just gotten up in court and told the judge that the Daddy was a victim of cultural miscommunication, I all of a sudden wished it were Mr. Hollings and his grubby hands and perverted "heh-heh-heh" I was stuck in the elevator with.

"But it maybe rain this weekend," Ma said.

Then the elevator doors opened and Mr. Levinson said, "Well, let's hope that cools things down some."

"Oh yes, heh-heh."

"Heh-heh-heh."

Enid and I went out to the baking-hot parking lot and left Ma and Mr. Levinson in the lobby.

"The weather is so not funny," I said. "Except maybe if you're out having a picnic in a park and then you get this, like, sun-shower coming out of nowhere that soaks your hot dog buns and gets your soda all watery. And even then it's like an 'Oh, shit' funny, not a 'Ha, ha, ha,' pee-in-my-pants kind of funny. I'm never ever gonna laugh at stupid stuff when I grow up. I'm never gonna have any stupid kids and let myself get all fucking weird so they end up hating my guts 'cause I go around laughing at . . ."

Enid put her arms around my shoulders and said, "It's okay, Katu. I didn't tell the judge what really happened either."

I guess you could say that Enid and I could have prevented everything that happened after that day just by telling the judge the stuff that was going on in our house. No one was in those chambers with us but the judge. I went first, and then he called Enid in. No one was there to give us the evil eye or to pinch us if we started to say something that we shouldn't.

But then again, they didn't have to be in the room to be right there with us. Ma was there. The Daddy was there. Gran and Aunt Merlude were there. Augustin and Uncle Jude and Delta and the twins and Clara and the cop with his hand on his baton. They'd know what we had said by what the judge decided to do.

And who's to say that things would have been any better for anyone if we had told the truth that day, anyway? It's like if someone gets five numbers out of the lottery, just one number away from a gazillion dollars, then they spend forever beating themselves up and thinking if they'd just picked their birthday day instead of their birthday month, then they'd be driving, like, a Lamborghini and living in a palace with, like, a swimming pool and a butler in a tuxedo. But what if they had picked their birthday day and then hit the jackpot? Who's to say they wouldn't have just dropped dead of a heart attack from the shock of it all? Or gotten hit by a bus on their way to picking up their giant check?

Sure, lots of messed-up things happened after that day in court, but you know, there are some things that ended up happening that I wouldn't have wanted *not* to happen. And maybe those good things that happened wouldn't have if we had told the truth.

Gran was putting lunch out onto the kitchen table when I walked into the house. Delta ran up to me and asked, "What happened, Katu?"

I didn't answer.

Delta looked over my shoulder when she heard the front door slam shut, then she spun around and ran through the kitchen and out the back door, yelling, "I hate you, Karina Marie Lamond! I swear to God, I hate you!"

It occurred to me right then that Delta had still held out hope that I would tell the truth and make things right. Though if I would lie to a priest, I don't know what made her think I wouldn't lie to a judge.

When the Daddy walked into the kitchen, Gran said, "*Bon jou*, Monsieur Gaston." She said it in a tone that made the Daddy think twice about going over to embrace her.

He mumbled, "*Bon jou,*" and left the kitchen.

Delta didn't come in for lunch, and Gran didn't call her. Enid stayed in Aunt Merlude's room. Gran piled the food on our plates like we had to eat for everyone who wasn't there, even Ma and the Daddy. The twins and I ate up everything on our plates and didn't complain.

I found a plastic grocery bag on my pillow when I went up to my room. Inside were three one-subject spiral notebooks. One green, one red, one yellow. There was a box of brand-new yellow number two pencils and a tiny little yellow pencil sharpener. I pulled out the piece of paper sticking out of the green notebook. On one side my mom had printed in her blocky, shaky handwriting, "FOR YOU BETDAY." On the other side was the receipt from the pharmacy. Five dollars and seventy-six cents for my birthday presents. Five dollars and seventy-six cents' worth of stuff for letting the Daddy come back into the house. I stuck the bag under my bed, changed out of my church clothes, and went down to see Augustin.

"Daddy's back home," I said, like Augustin could have possibly missed three hundred extra pounds stomping around above his head.

He nodded.

"I had to go speak to the judge to tell him to let Daddy come back home." I took Marcus's picture down and lay across Augustin's bed. "If Marcus comes to America, will you both live here together?"

Augustin usually turned the radio off when I came down to talk to him, but he hadn't done so yet and didn't hear me. I rolled over and turned the radio volume down.

"I explained to the judge and all the lawyers and everyone in court that we could only stay in this house with you and everybody else if Daddy came home to drive his taxi and pay the bills and that he couldn't just make us all homeless and put us on welfare and send you and Aunt Merlude back to Haiti just because of a dumb fight I had with Enid. Are you listening to me, Augustin?"

"*Oui*, Katu," he said.

"Are you glad Daddy is back?"

"*Oui*," he said. "*Oui*."

I didn't know what had made Augustin and the Daddy friends when they were growing up in Haiti. I rarely saw the Daddy go down into the basement to hang out with Augustin. But obviously Augustin thought the Daddy wasn't too bad of a guy. Maybe the Daddy was really an okay person once upon a time.

It took a couple of days before Delta would talk to me again. I got up early the morning after court when I heard her getting dressed to go to Tuesday-morning Mass and offered to walk her to the church. She always asked me to walk her because not many people were out that early on summer weekdays, and she was afraid of running into Mr. Hollings by herself. Most of the time I said no. Once in a while she'd beg so much that I'd go with her, but only one block past Mr. Hollings's house.

That morning, though, I told her I'd take her all the way to the chapel, and I pulled on a pair of jeans over my pajamas as she walked out of the room. She wasn't waiting for me outside the front door like she did sometimes even when I told her I wouldn't go. I walked out to the edge of the front yard and spotted her two blocks up already. She was running.

15.

The more I went over to the community center, the bolder Rachael and I got about dodging work. Rachael and I decided to hide out in the day-care room one entire day to see if anyone noticed. Laurel had really begun to get on my case about sitting with some of the center's Haitian clients and helping them with paperwork—like explaining to them which number on their telephone bill was how much they had to pay and how to fill in a check, and calling the electric company and making a payment plan so their lights could be turned back on.

Even though the center was pretty stupid when it came to something easy like the difference between punishing kids and torturing them, the staff really did some cool stuff for people who couldn't speak English. And I really wanted to help, too, and I did a few times, but to tell the truth, hanging out with Rachael was getting to be way more fun.

Not that she actually liked me yet. It was more like I was one of the poor "no 'peak de English" alien kids who got dragged into the center all the time, but instead of just staring and wondering, she could ask me all sorts of questions she had wanted to ask them, because after all, I did speak the English.

By the time I was sitting at dinner with her family that first time I visited her house, and she had her hand at her mouth giggling as Laurel explained that I should place the napkin in my lap and pointed out which was the salad fork and which was the soup spoon, I'd already decided that Rachael would become my first real best friend. In return I'd let her treat me as her very own pet project. She could tug on my kinky hair, make me teach her curses in Creole, look at the undersides of my feet to see if they were the same color as my skin or the same color as the palms of my hands. I'd even make up gibberish words and show her funny dances and tell her it was a voodoo spell we could put on her parents so they'd never ground her again. I didn't think it was that bad a trade-off. I don't know what Rachael thought because I didn't exactly tell her of our little deal.

We sat in one corner of the day-care room, magazines opened up all around us, scissors and glue and construction paper in hand. We were supposed to be finishing up collages to decorate the day-care center room, and if Bethel or Laurel or Mr. Levinson came busting in, that's just what it would look like we were doing. But really Rachael was telling me just how she planned on losing her virginity and who she was going to lose it to, and I was sniffing at her hair. It smelled like strawberries and floor wax, but mostly like strawberries.

"What are you doing?" Rachael asked in the middle of her story.

"Just listening," I said.

"With your tongue in my hair, you total freak?"

"Why do you put strawberries in your hair?"

"Oh. My. *God.* It's called shampoo?"

"How do you plan on losing your virginity if you're grounded?"

"Did your parents, like, drop you on your head a lot when you were a baby?"

"Yeah," I laughed.

"No wonder," laughed Rachael. "I'm not going to do it while I'm grounded. I mean, I could just sneak out my window. . . ."

"With a ladder, I hope."

"It's not really as far down as it looks. Jump, tuck, and roll. At least six years of gymnastics class were good for something."

"So why not do it now?"

"Because I'm not ready," said Rachael. She gave me a look like that should have been obvious or something.

"So you're not ready to have sex now, but you will be next week? What's gonna happen by then?"

"You don't understand," she said, and rolled her eyes. "You're such a baby."

"I'm going into eighth grade and you're going into ninth, so it's not like you're as old as my mom. Get over yourself," I said. "Besides, I don't know what's so hot about running into the arms of your lover boy, all limping and sweaty and grass stained from cartwheeling outta your bedroom window to be with him. So romantic!"

"Not so loud," said Rachael as she slapped my leg. "I'm not going to jump out the window. When I'm off punishment, Seth and I are going to ask to go to the movies, but instead he's gonna drop me off at Larry's, and he's gonna go see Brandi."

"Ewww! His name is Larry?"

"So?"

"Actually, it's even more icky that your brother is going to pretend to go to the movies so you can do this," I realized.

"He owes me," said Rachael.

"Must be big," I answered.

Rachael took a deep breath. "Remember I told you why I was grounded in the first place? Well, the joints weren't mine."

"Why'd you take the blame for Seth?"

Rachael only shrugged and flicked her finger at some magazines on her lap.

"You let your parents think you're a drug addict, you get grounded for something you didn't even do, you don't get to see your friends for almost a whole summer, and you don't even know why?" I asked.

There had to be a story behind that one. There's a real good story behind every dumb thing that happens in life, and an even better story about the dumb people who do them. But Rachael wasn't giving it up.

No one did bother us during our day of pretend work at the center, and when closing time came, Mr.

Levinson asked me over for dinner again. I asked if Mrs. Levinson was making knishes this time. She was. So I went.

"Owww! Owwww!" Delta was sitting on the floor in the kitchen screaming at the top of her lungs. Enid sat in a chair behind her, trying to get the kinks out of Delta's hair.

"Do it slower, Fee Fee," I pleaded. It was my turn next, and even though Enid had just started with Delta, she'd already begun to get frustrated. At the rate she was going, she'd be ready to snap someone's neck just when it was my turn to sit in front of her.

It was a Saturday night in August. A few days after the Daddy came back home, he decided Enid was faking still being injured to get out of housework, and so he sent Gran back to Brooklyn. The Daddy stayed away from the house an awful lot, and when he was home, he didn't hit us, at least not the girls. Gerald and even Roland were getting smacked on the legs and on the butt a whole lot more than they used to. But really, as usual, Enid got the worse deal. Ma had started working more Saturday nights, so on top of getting back her house chores, she now had to get us all church ready.

The first couple of times Enid had to do our hair, she was real nice about it and just brushed around the three fat cornrows Delta and I had been wearing since Ma did our hair previously. But Enid used a wet brush, which took out the hot-combing Ma had done, and she eventually noticed how messy our heads were.

Now we had almost three weeks' worth of kinks that needed to be combed out, and no amount of Dax that Enid smeared onto our heads was going to make the job any less painful. Ma really should have just washed our hair, but she was mad that Enid hadn't done as she was told, and so she decided we'd all just suffer the consequences and learn our lesson that way.

Delta and I had hair like Ma used to have before she got it relaxed. It was long and thick and as tangled as an old, used-up scouring pad. Enid must have gotten her hair from her father's side of the family. It never grew very long, and it was soft and almost not curly at all. She never had massive kinks to hack through, but it still didn't escape my notice that with the condition her hair was in, she must have been taking it out of its ponytail every day and greasing and combing it. She always smelled of lemongrass and honey lately.

"You could've reminded us to comb out our hair too, you know," I said to her.

"You're fourteen years old now, Katu!" Enid had to yell to be heard over Delta's crying. "Does someone really have to remind you to comb your damned hair every once in a while?"

Enid got fed up with all the squirming and finally pinned Delta between her knees. One knee was pressed up against Delta's spine, the other against her chest.

"I can't breathe, Fee Fee!"

"You wouldn't be able to talk if you couldn't breathe," said Enid as a tooth from the comb broke off and flew across the room.

"Don't break her neck," I said. Then I went up to Ma's bathroom to get the big bottle of aspirin.

I'd been going to the community center twice a week, sometimes three times. I never went on Tuesdays and Thursdays, though, because those were the afternoons when the Daddy had to go to his class at the center, and I didn't want to run into him. Most times I went to the center, Mr. Levinson would drive me to his house for dinner before taking me back home. Rachael stopped complaining about it.

The last time I was at the center, I told Mr. Levinson that I couldn't come over for dinner because my mom wanted me home early for Gerald's birthday dinner. Rachael actually looked upset, and Mr. Levinson noticed. He asked if I thought Ma would let me have a sleepover with Rachael, and Ma said it was okay.

That was the only reason I was about to sit in front of Enid and let her torture me. The next day after church the Daddy would drive me to Rachael's house, and I would spend the night and most of Monday. I had packed the very day I found out I was going, but before Ma left for work that Saturday, she unpacked my shorts and T-shirts and put in two dresses, a brand-new nightgown, and three pairs of new underwear. I was too excited to care.

Then she handed me this long baby-blue ribbon that had a small pouch and a loop on each end. I had no idea what it was, but I said, "Thank you, Ma," and stuffed it into my bag.

"Put it on to see if it fits," she said.

"Put it on where?" I asked after looking it over and deciding it was too thin to be a scarf and too thick to be shoelaces.

Ma shook her head and said, "Take off your shirt."

She grabbed my left arm and put it through one of the loops, then wrapped the ribbon around my back and came up to my other side and put my right arm through the other loop. Then she took the edges of the pouches and pulled them together at my chest and snapped them in place. I looked down at my very first bra. The pouches looked like deflated balloons.

"It's the smallest size they have," said Ma. "You'll grow into them."

"Maybe I can just wear it when it fits," I said. *Like when my boobs get bigger than Gerald's, maybe?*

"You can't go to strangers' house looking like a baby," said Ma. "Wear it every day when you're there."

"Even when I'm sleeping?"

Ma sucked her teeth and shook her head. "Dummy."

"Your turn, Katu!" Delta was banging on the bathroom door. I heard her try the doorknob. "What are you doing in there?"

"I'm taking a bath," I said.

"Why are you *always* taking a bath now even when nobody tells you to, Katu?"

I didn't answer, and next thing I knew, Delta was running down the stairs, yelling, "Fee Fee, Katu has a boyfriend!"

"I do not have a boyfriend," I said as I followed Delta

into the kitchen, still dripping from my bath. Enid was sitting in the same place, her feet on tiptoes, an elbow on her knee, chin in hand.

"I asked if you're ready for me to comb your hair," she said.

Delta stood next to Enid, her eyes bloody red from all the crying. "Did you get everything clean for your boyfriend?"

I could tell she wanted to laugh at me, but the skin on her face was so purply raw and tight from having all the hair on her head stretched into tiny cornrow braids and pulled into a ponytail that she could only giggle a little, and even then she had to hold her head with both hands.

Enid reached over and slapped Delta's shoulder lightly with the comb. "Find something else to do, Dee Dee," she said.

Delta said, "You didn't all of a sudden start taking a bath twice a day when you got a boyfriend. How come Katu does?"

I tried to turn and look at Delta, but Enid had my head pinned between her elbow and her thigh.

"So you do have a boyfriend, Fee Fee," I said between groans.

"Yup, she does," said Delta.

Enid said, "Shut up, Dee Dee." But even though I had one ear pressed down against her lap, I swear I could tell Enid was smiling when she said it.

Delta came around and sat in front of me. "His name is Mickey, and he's not black and he's not American."

"That's none of your business, you two, and it's not true," said Enid.

"He's Haitian?" I asked.

"Hell no, he's not Haitian," answered Enid.

Delta and I laughed. "Wait," I said. "Isn't that your friend whose sister's going to Harvard?"

"He's Russian," said Delta.

"How do you know stuff like that?" asked Enid.

"Is she right?" I asked. I long ago stopped caring that Delta knew things and figured out things before I did. I just didn't like it when she kept the things she knew a secret from me for too long.

"Because that time he called here, he sounded like my friend Anna's mom," said Delta.

"That's enough blabbing about my life, Dee Dee," said Enid.

After we'd had our hair done and Enid was up in bed, Delta and I pieced together enough—from phone calls and extra time on hair combing to all that volunteering she'd do to help Aunt Merlude at the Mrs.'s house—to fill in all the blanks about Enid's hot love affair with a Russian guy already old enough to be out of high school and drive his own car. We spent so much time making up stories about Enid's secret boyfriend that Delta forgot all about making fun of me because of mine.

16.

Rachael was already under the covers when I stepped out of the bathroom in my new pink and gray nightgown. She lay flat on her back, the covers pulled up to her chin, her head turned to the television. She laughed hysterically as Jack Tripper on *Three's Company* stubbed his toe on a table leg, then got slammed in the head with the swinging kitchen door. Rachael turned her head and laughed even harder when she saw me.

"What the hell is that on your head?" she asked.

"I don't want my hair all messed up," I said as I patted at my head scarf.

"Yeah, so what's the deal with your grandmother's nightgown?"

I shrugged. "My mom just got it for me. I don't like it all that much, but whatever."

"Looks like she bought it at Sears," said Rachael.

Of course my mom had bought it at Sears. She'd shop there if she wanted something nice. But to Rachael, who only shopped at the mall, Sears was a place for poor people. Even though I hated pink and I hated nightgowns and I hated anything that looked like a dress, Ma was only trying not to let me look like some kind of welfare case in front of Rachael's fancy-ass family.

Rachael's laughing finally started to die down, and in the TV light my eyes started to focus on a new piece of furniture in her room. It was a cot opened up next to her bed.

"What is that?" I asked, though I knew.

"That's where you're sleeping," said Rachael.

I pulled my arms out of the nightgown sleeves then pulled the whole thing over my head. I was wearing normal-people sleeping clothes underneath—shorts and a T-shirt. I left my new nightgown on the floor by the bathroom door, jumped onto Rachael's footlocker, and bounced into her bed.

"God! What are you doing?"

"I think this bed is big enough for two people," I said. "Fact, I could fit myself and all my brothers and sisters on this bed."

"All my sleepovers stay on the cot."

"Bullshit," I said.

"What?"

"I don't believe you, that's what."

I noticed then that Rachael hadn't loosened her grip on her blanket since I stepped out of the bathroom. I yanked on it suddenly but didn't fool her; she held on tight. I straddled her waist and let my full weight fall onto her stomach.

"Let me see what you're wearing or I'll tickle you until you pee," I said.

"Go lock the door," she whispered.

By the time I'd done that, Rachael was out from underneath the covers, turning on the lamp at her bedside table. She was fully dressed. And not in the jeans and T-shirt she'd been wearing earlier that day, but in a miniskirt and a nice shirt, the kind with two straps you tie together behind your neck and no sleeves to stick your arms through.

"Where are you going?"

"To a party," said Rachael as she began pulling makeup out of the drawers of her vanity table.

"A party on a Sunday night?" I asked. The outfit was nice, but I was staring hard at the makeup, hoping she wasn't planning on turning herself into the Boy George look-alike she'd been when I first met her.

"There're only a couple weekends left before school starts again," she explained.

"I don't want to go," I said.

I was disappointed with Rachael and surprised at myself. I should have been thrilled for a chance to go to a party with kids my age. The chance wasn't ever likely to come up again. Even though I lived on the other side of town and wouldn't be going to the same high school as Rachael, I might still meet kids who'd be going to my high school. Then they'd know me as a cool person who snuck away from home to go to parties in the middle of the night, and I'd actually have friends to hang out with before the school year really got under way and they started avoiding me when I started acting like, well, me again.

But I wasn't thrilled about anything. I didn't want

to meet any new kids. I didn't realize how much I really wanted to spend a lot of time alone with Rachael and how pissed off I'd get when she tried to ruin it. I thought of blowing the whistle on her, but then, that was just dumb—she'd get grounded and I'd probably have to leave.

"Just don't put on too much makeup," I said. "Like, you don't need eye shadow or even blush, really."

"No way, I have to have blush. A little, okay?"

"So why are you hanging out with your real friends again?" I asked.

"My real friends?"

"Yeah, you know, people other than me. I know you've only been putting up with me 'cause you were grounded."

Rachael shook her head. "That's not true," she said.

But I didn't really believe her. Making fun of her mom was bonding experience enough for, like, the first two times I hung out at her house. But then that got boring, and we'd just talk about dumb stuff and watch TV, and she'd put on makeup and I'd tell her how much was way too much and she'd wipe it off and put it back on. I didn't mind. But I've watched enough television shows to know that rich kids with real lives get to do way more exciting stuff than that.

"Did you get grounded again and not tell me?" I asked.

"I didn't get grounded again," said Rachael.

"And you didn't go sneak off and lose your virginity," I said. "I would've noticed that."

"Huh?"

"You would've been walking different afterward," I said.

"That's so gross!" said Rachael.

It might have been gross, but I had gotten that piece of sex ed straight from Miss Smarty-pants. Rachael sat in front of her vanity and started powdering her cheeks with blush.

"Enough!" I yelled.

"Eyeliner?"

"You don't need it."

"Lipstick," she said as she pulled out a hideously neon pink tube.

I grabbed the tube of lipstick from her and handed her another. "Lip gloss," I said.

I brushed her hair, and brushed and brushed it some more, until Rachael was convinced she didn't need hair spray.

"Okay, what are you going to wear?"

"I don't really want to go," I said. "Besides, I've never taken gymnastics, and I'm not jumping out of any windows."

Rachael went through my bag, pulled out the two dresses, made a face, and let them fall to the floor. She went into her closet and started looking through her outfits.

"I don't have anything for your bigfoot feet, but this should fit you," she said.

"No way," I said. "I don't do miniskirts."

"And you can wear this on top," she said as she

tossed the miniskirt onto the bed and pulled out a matching shirt.

"Didn't you hear me?" I asked.

"Just try it on and see," she said as I rolled my eyes. "You don't have to go anywhere if you don't want to. I mean, if you want to be totally lame, that's fine by me."

I dropped my shorts and pulled on the miniskirt. It fit perfectly.

"I guess we're the same size," I said as I pulled my T-shirt off over my head.

I heard Rachael gasp. "Is that a surgery scar?" she asked.

"Nope," I said.

"What happened?"

"I'll give you three guesses," I said as Rachael walked over to me. "No, make that just one guess."

Rachael reached out and ran her index finger from my side to my belly button, and I thought I had been electrocuted in the crotch. I pushed her hand away.

"It feels all rubbery," she said.

"Give me the shirt," I said as I quietly counted to ten and started to sweat.

"What are we going to do with your hair?"

"Oh, we are doing absolutely nothing with my hair," I said. I'd already given Rachael the speech about black girls' hair versus white girls' hair several times.

"I know, I know, but . . ."

"It took my sister almost two hours to untangle and braid it."

"But you never wear it any other way except maybe

pigtails, which are sooo first grade, and I was thinking since, umm . . ."

"Since?"

"Since you actually look like a girl now, maybe—"

"I look like a girl *now*?"

". . . we could try something new with your hair—"

"What did I look like before?"

". . . like let it out or something."

"Bubble gum," I said.

"What?"

"Your lip gloss smells like bubble gum."

"I could have told you that," said Rachael. "You don't have to stand so close."

But just after she said I shouldn't stand so close to her, she stuck her face in mine and kissed me on the mouth. I know what you're thinking. I passed out again and imagined it all. Or maybe I imagined it all and then passed out. Well, for a second I thought that too. I didn't move. I didn't try to kiss back. Not that I would've known how anyway. I just waited for someone to start shouting for me to get up off the floor. But that didn't happen.

She really did kiss me. It was absolutely the weirdest and nicest and scariest and happiest moment of my entire life, and it lasted forever and was over in a split second when she stepped away from me and picked up the lip gloss tube.

"You can wear some if you like it," she said.

It wasn't until after she said that that I heard someone shouting for me to get up off the floor. Rachael stared down at me with her mouth hanging open.

"I'll go get my mom," she said, and started to walk away.

I grabbed her leg. "Then she'll ask why you're all dressed up," I said.

"You're scaring the shit outta me, Karina!"

"Sorry," I said. "I . . . I have a condition and it just happens sometimes."

"You have epilepsy?" she asked.

"Yeah, I think so," I said. I'd heard of epilepsy before, and it sounded like a fine thing to have just then, but Rachael punched me in the shoulder.

"You *think* so?"

I shrugged and sat up.

"You freaked because I kissed you, didn't you?" Rachael whispered.

"Why'd you do that?"

She shrugged. "Just felt like it, I guess."

"Are you ever going to feel like it again?" I asked. "'Cause maybe next time you could warn me first."

I looked around me. Rachael's bedroom was a heck of a lot better place to pass out in than most places I'd done it before. Lots of open space and a nice fluffy carpet to land on. But we'd been standing kinda close to the vanity when she kissed me, and my arm must have caught on the leg of her chair or table or something. My wrist was beginning to throb.

I got up and sat on her footlocker, rubbing my wrist. Rachael started to sit next to me but changed her mind and sat at her vanity table.

"You sure you're okay?" she asked.

I nodded, and for a while we did nothing but try to avoid looking at each other.

Finally Rachael said, "I don't really want to do it with Larry."

"Who says you have to?" I asked.

"That's why I told my parents the joints were mine."

Jeez, she was as good at telling stories as Delta. I frowned at her.

"Seth and I were at this party, and they were playing seven in heaven, and when it was my turn with Larry, I didn't want to do it. And my friends were like, 'Oh, you're so lame, you're such a baby, you're a tease,' blah, blah, blah. So when my mom found pot in the car the next day and asked whose it was, I just said it was mine, 'cause I knew I'd be grounded forever and wouldn't have to make up stupid excuses not to hang out with my so-called friends anymore."

"But all of a sudden you were going to lose your virginity to him?" I asked.

"Then everyone would stop making fun of me and I wouldn't be some, like, friendless dork for the rest of my life," she said. Then after a long second she added, "Like you."

"Gee, let me see," I said, playing all prim and proper. "On this hand I could be a friendless dork forever, and on this other hand I could let some guy I don't like shove his thing up in me so my friends will think I'm cool. Gee, whatever will I do?"

"It wouldn't be so funny if you'd ever had a friend

in your life or ever even had the chance to have one," said Rachael.

"You know what your problem is?" I said. "You're a spoiled brat. You're so used to your fancy clothes and your fancy parties and your fancy friends that you'd have a cow if you ever thought it would all go away."

"I'm the one who got grounded on purpose so I wouldn't have to spend time with my fancy friends, stupid."

"And you're the one who spent your whole punishment time trying to figure out how to make them like you again," I said. "And then the best you come up with is letting some icky guy stick his thing up—"

"Stop saying that!"

It was so weird with Rachael, because even when she was mean to me, I didn't really like being mean back to her. It felt like I had to try too hard, and even when I got her good, it didn't feel good. We went back to avoiding eye contact for a few moments.

"You know, why didn't you just do seven in heaven with someone else?" I asked after a while. "I mean, I've never played, but can't you just pick who you want to make out with?"

Rachael shook her head, then said, "Besides, I don't think they would've let me pick the person I wanted."

Rachael had been real serious right after I passed out, and then I got her all pissed off, but now I could tell she was trying hard not to laugh. Her eyebrows kept twitching, and she sucked in her cheeks and lips like she had just eaten a whole chunk of lemon.

"Who?" I asked, laughing.

She put her finger to her lips, then sat beside me on the footlocker and whispered in my ear as if someone could overhear us.

"No way!" I shouted. "Isn't that your brother's girl-friend?"

"Shut up!" said Rachael in a loud whisper. "And you can't tell Seth. Or anybody."

"I don't even talk to Seth, like, ever."

"I mean, I know it's weird for girls to make out with other girls, but I dunno, I just *wanted* to," she said.

And then for some reason, don't ask me why, I fell back onto the bed and started laughing my head off. Rachael kept trying to shush me, slapping at me and holding a pillow over my face. But I laughed and laughed and laughed, rolling from one side of her bed to the other. I laughed until tears were pouring down my face and I thought I'd either pee or throw up.

I sat up finally, panting for breath and wiping tears and snot onto my bare arms. Rachael stood by the bedroom door, slowly hyperventilating and looking absolutely terrified.

"You know who I wanted to kiss?" I asked.

"Who?" said Rachael as she moved away from the door.

"Suzanne."

"Isn't that a girl's name?"

"Duh."

"So, did you do it?" asked Rachael. She didn't look

too terrified anymore, and her breathing was calming down.

"I came close," I said. "A couple of times."

"Close?" Rachael sat on the edge of the bed.

"Well, I kinda passed out and knocked her down a couple of times."

Now it was Rachael's turn to laugh her head off. While she did, I went into the bathroom and washed my arms and face and put my shorts and T-shirt back on. Rachael was in her pajamas when I came back into the bedroom. I looked at the cot, then looked at Rachael. She shrugged. I climbed into the bed next to her and pulled the covers up.

"Don't tell anyone about what we did tonight, okay?"

"Okay," I answered.

"Promise?"

"Promise."

"Tell me how this happened," she said.

Before I could ask what she was talking about, Rachael had her hand in my shirt and was touching my scar again. I pulled her hand out and held on to it.

"You gotta try and stay as still as you can when a belt is coming at you," I said. "I mean, you can't help but jump once it hits you, but before that you gotta stand still."

I felt Rachael try to pull her hand out of mine. I held it tighter.

"One wrong move and the edge of the belt gets you, and it's just like a knife."

"My dad used to be a regular lawyer in the city," she

said. "Then one day in court he had a heart attack, and the doctors said he might die."

"Really?"

"When he got out of the hospital, he quit his regular job and opened up the center."

"Why?"

"He said that he'd always wanted to help people, and when he thought he was dying, he was sad because all he did was go to court for these big, giant companies and make them a ton of money and that's not what he was meant to do with his life."

"But he still makes money," I said.

"Not really," said Rachael. "My mom got all this money when my granddad died. That's the only reason she let my dad quit the law firm."

"But she's so into it," I said.

"She always used to do volunteer work, but I think she likes it more now since she's rich and she knows she's never gonna be like the people she helps."

"That's weird."

"I'm gonna tell my dad the truth about your stepfather, Karina," said Rachael.

"Why bother?" I asked. "I bet deep down he already knows the truth."

"He isn't like that," said Rachael. "He'd do something, especially if he found out about you passing out all over the place. I know you didn't do that because I kissed you."

"Just don't tell your father anything," I said.

"Why not?"

"Just don't," I said. "It'll make things worse."

"But what if something is really wrong with you, Karina?"

"There's nothing wrong with me, okay? So promise you won't tell."

Rachael didn't answer.

"Promise?" I said again.

"Promise," said Rachael.

"Thanks," I said. Then I closed my eyes and asked, "Do you want to kiss again?"

"You're not going to pass out again, are you?"

"I might," I said. "But I'm already lying down."

Rachael wiggled her hand out of mine. As she inched toward me, my heartbeats were like someone punching me in the ears. It seemed to take forever for her lips to reach mine.

I didn't faint, though.

17.

Out of the clear blue sky a couple mornings later Ma came into our room and told me and Delta to go clean Uncle Jude's apartment after we had our breakfast. It was the first time we'd been asked to go since the Daddy came back from jail. We had reminded Ma almost every week, until she got annoyed and said that Uncle Jude didn't want us there anymore.

Uncle Jude was disappointed that I didn't tell the judge what happened to Enid. He was disappointed that his own brother didn't end up in jail forever. That's what I figured. And right then I loved Uncle Jude a little less than I had loved him before. How could he be mad at me when he was a grown-up and wouldn't do anything about the Daddy except make an anonymous phone call, then hide out in his apartment getting drunk?

When we got to his apartment, Uncle Jude threw open the doors and yelled, "My sweethearts!"

He grabbed me by the shoulders, kissed my forehead over and over again, then hugged me tight. Then he did the same to Delta. Uncle Jude stank of beer and wine and cigarettes and sweat, but he sure was happy. It seemed like he'd forgiven me for what happened in court with the Daddy, but I was still peeved at him. He would make up for it, though, a thousand times over, the night the Daddy died.

The apartment was a total pigsty and smelled like cigarette smoke and feet. There were empty beer cans absolutely everywhere. Rumpled sheets were piled on the couch, and the coffee table was full of plates with crusted food, dirty drinking glasses, beer cans, wine bottles, cigarette butts, and lots of other crap I couldn't even identify. Underneath the coffee table and scattered around the rest of the living room were empty pizza boxes and Styrofoam containers from the Haitian bakery and restaurant.

Uncle Jude had obviously been using the living room as bedroom and kitchen for a while. It kinda made sense 'cause he didn't have a television in his actual bedroom.

"I go out for little bit," said Uncle Jude as he patted himself down, trying to find his car keys.

"Where are you going?" I asked.

"Cigarette store," he answered. "You see my key?"

"No," said Delta. "But it's nice outside, you should just walk."

Uncle Jude laughed. "I no need exercise," he said. He was slurring pretty badly now. "Your daddy need diet, no me."

Uncle Jude started to fling the sheets off the couch and onto the floor, and then he shuffled through a stack of unopened mail on the kitchen counter. Delta and I each got a garbage bag out from underneath the sink and started filling them up. Uncle Jude seemed to have forgotten about the cigarettes and was cursing at a bill he'd pulled from an envelope.

"Can we put on the radio?" I asked.

Uncle Jude looked up finally and said, "Okay, I walk. Clean good, my sweethearts, and find my key."

"It'll take forever and a day to find anything in here," I said after he left.

"Not really," said Delta as she pulled her shirt out of her jeans with her left hand and caught Uncle Jude's key with her right.

"When did you do that?" I laughed.

"I saw it on the floor right near the door when he was hugging and kissing you."

"Good job, Dee Dee," I said, and slapped her high five.

When Delta turned on the radio, they were right in the middle of her favorite song, and after we'd finished jumping around the apartment singing, "'Wake me up before you go-go!'" we turned the radio down just a little and got back to cleaning.

Cleaning up at Uncle Jude's wasn't like cleaning up at home. We did basically the same stuff as at home, like throw out the garbage, wash the dishes, sweep and mop the floors. But Uncle Jude wasn't picky like Ma and didn't go over every crack and corner to see if we'd missed anything. As long as the apartment looked better than he'd left it and we managed to get the stink out as best we could, Uncle Jude was happy. Plus, when we cleaned his place, we got to blast the radio and act like the Solid Gold Dancers.

Like I said earlier, last year Delta and I found an almost full bottle of red wine underneath the sink and decided to try it out. We'd seen his wine bottles before, but that day was just after Delta and I got our first Communion, and we wanted to know if Uncle Jude's wine tasted like the blood of Christ. It did pretty much. We kept sipping from it and playing Uncle Jude's *Thriller* record over and over and dancing and singing and giggling and cleaning. Pretty soon we were just sipping and giggling.

Uncle Jude came home and freaked out. We were drunk and his apartment was messier than when he'd left it. He called Ma and told her that we had done such a good job cleaning that he wanted us to stay over and watch a movie on cable TV. We didn't watch any movie, though, since Uncle Jude hadn't paid his bill and his cable got cut off. Delta and I woke up the next morning in Uncle Jude's bed, and we were sick as dogs. From then on Uncle Jude hid his wine when we came over to clean.

We were pretty much done with the kitchen and living room when Delta took out the Michael Jackson record and propped it on a windowsill and started to sing "Every Breath You Take" to him. The empty beer bottle Delta was using for a microphone would whistle with every breath she took, 'cause she held it so close to her mouth. Uncle Jude still hadn't returned from getting his cigarettes, so I decided to go into his bedroom and see if it needed cleaning.

We didn't usually clean up in there, and even Ma

had told us to stay out of his bedroom unless he asked for it to be cleaned. But I wanted to buy something for Rachael, and I figured I might be able to if I could get Uncle Jude to give us more than the five bucks he usually did even though Ma told him not to pay us. That kinda pissed me off. I mean, I *loved* Uncle Jude and everything, but it was the 1980s, not the 1780s. Abraham Lincoln outlawed slavery a long time ago.

The bed was unmade and there were clothes thrown around on the floor, but this room was nowhere near as messy as the others. Still, I figured I could make it look even better. I picked up all his clothing and gave each a quick sniff. Whatever didn't smell I hung in the closet or folded away into his dresser drawers. The smelly stuff I piled near the doorway. Underwear and socks went on the pile automatically. I so wasn't gonna sniff those.

On the top shelf of the closet I noticed the clean sheets Delta and I had folded that summer day we last cleaned up Uncle Jude's apartment, and I realized that he hadn't changed his sheets since then. Pretty damn gross, right? I stripped his bed of the old sheets and remade the bed with the clean ones. When I lifted one of the mattress corners to tuck the sheet in, my hand brushed against something and I pulled it out. Guess what it was.

Remember a few years ago when everyone was so happy because of the first black Miss America ever, but then they made her give back the crown 'cause someone found dirty pictures of her? Well, the magazine

Uncle Jude had under his mattress was filled with dirty pictures of Miss America. I won't tell you what she was doing exactly in those pictures. I'll just say they were *soooo* nasty.

Uncle Jude was happy with the job we'd done with his apartment. He gave each of us five dollars, and when I pointed out that I'd also cleaned his bedroom, he gave me another five. I had fifteen dollars to spend on something for Rachael because Delta had given me her share, since I'd finally told her that Seth was my boyfriend and now she thought we had another great big secret together.

The next weekend I had another sleepover at Rachael's. I handed her a shoe box that I'd wrapped in Christmas paper.

"Duh," she said. "I'm Jewish."

"Duh," I said back to her. "It's not Christmas and that's the only wrapping paper I could find at my house."

"Why are you giving me a present? Happy End of Summer Vacation?"

"Just open it."

She tore open the paper and held up the shoe box. "Shoes from Sears?"

"Very funny," I said.

She opened the lid, undid all the toilet paper wrapping inside, and pulled out five small plastic boy dolls. She started laughing.

"It's Menudo!" I said.

"How do you know?"

"That's what that tiny writing on their shirts says."

"Oh."

"This is Roy, that's Robby, and there's Ray," I said. "And I always get those other two mixed up."

"This is so . . ."

"What?"

"It's cool," she said finally. "Thanks."

Each little doll stood on its own round stage, and Rachael lined them up on her windowsill. I guess she wasn't planning any more airborne gymnastics.

18.

School started back up again that Wednesday. With all the time I'd spent over the summer having fun with Rachael and being practically *relaxed* at home, I'd forgotten to get nervous about the start of another year of school until I walked into the building that morning. I had Mr. Rosenberg for my first few classes, but instead of going straight there, I took the back staircase around the corner from the cafeteria so that I'd purposely pass by the special-ed class. I did it to remind myself why I had to bring my grades up and do my homework every night no matter how much I hated to. It was like a form of self-discipline or self-punishment, I'm not sure.

I don't know what the connection is between special-ed kids and rodents and reptiles. The special-ed class at my old elementary school had this brown hamster in a cage that spent all day going round and round on a wheel, when it wasn't pooping or eating. And in the middle school the windowsills of the special-ed class were lined with glass cages with snakes and lizards and mice. Plus, those classes almost never have girls in them. Just huge black and Puerto Rican boys who are already growing mustaches and look older than some of the teachers. My cousin Edner told me that it was the same way when he was going to school in Brooklyn. He called special education the Class of Creeps and Critters.

Gorilla Arms Manning flapped his massive hands at me from his seat and made kissy noises so loud the rest of his class turned to stare at me. "I love you, Karina!" he yelled out in a pip-squeak voice. He turned to one of his retard classmates and said loudly, "That's my girlfriend!"

As I made my way down the hall, I heard the retard classmate say, "Man, that weirdo is yo' girl?"

Mrs. Mahajan was standing outside her classroom and gave me a funny look like she was working up in her mind just what she'd tell the high school counselors so that they'd stick me in the special-ed class. I pretended not to see her.

Suzanne wasn't in any of my classes that year. I didn't see her until I went to take the bus. Number 23, the one Suzanne rode, was the same bus that went by the community center. Ma had given me permission to go to the community center once or twice a week after school, and I decided I wouldn't go on Tuesdays or Thursdays because, like I said before, those were the afternoons when the Daddy was at the center taking parenting classes.

I got on the bus and saw Suzanne. She saw me, too, and her eyes got big as saucers. I just ignored her. I could feel her turn and stare as I walked right by her down the aisle and sat all the way in the back. Maybe she thought

I was trying to follow her, or maybe she thought I'd ask why she didn't write me over the summer.

David rode the same bus, and he gave me a funny look when he got on and took the seat next to Suzanne. He whispered something to her, and they both laughed, then turned to stare at me. As the bus pulled away from the school parking lot, David ducked down in his seat. Suzanne's giggling got so loud I could hear it over everyone else's yelling and the bus engine. Then David came back up as if he were yawning, his arms stretching over and behind his head. Suddenly something came flying out of his hand, bounced off the window behind me, and landed next to me on the seat. It was the glitter pen I'd given to Suzanne at the end of the previous year.

Suzanne just could not stop her giggling fit. And then it seemed that everyone on the bus was in on the joke and laughing along with her and looking my way. I didn't care, really I didn't. I mean, it's not like the pen clocked me in the head or something. Besides, little did Suzanne know I now had a friend way cooler than she could ever be with her glossy lips and sparkly braces and "Oh God, Karina!'s" and goo-goo eyes at David. What total dorks—the both of them.

Delta had started calling Tuesdays and Thursdays freedom days, since those were the days the Daddy went to the community center and came home the latest. Ma wasn't taking as many overtime shifts as in the beginning of the summer when we were all making plans for a life without the Daddy, so every once in a while she, too, would be home before him. On the first freedom day that was also a school day, Delta and I got home to find Ma in the kitchen preparing dinner. Enid was helping. Enid had gotten well enough to start school right on schedule. She'd said that even if she'd had to go in a wheelchair, she would have done it, though. It was her senior year, and nothing was going to prevent her from graduating on time, she'd said.

After all us kids had sat down to eat, Ma took out a folding chair from the hall closet and brought it into the kitchen. She left again and came back with a square plastic bucket filled with her manicure and pedicure stuff. I don't know why Ma bothered painting her nails, especially her fingernails. The polish never lasted more than a couple of days because of the boxes and the bottles she had to haul around at the factory. Ma sat with her feet soaking in the bucket and held her hand arched just above her thigh. She drew the brush in and out of the nail polish bottle sitting on the corner of the table and stroked it across her fingers very slowly, as if this time the Red Grape on her fingernails would be permanent.

"Can we watch TV, Ma?" I asked.

Jack and Joseph looked at me hopefully. Ma said, "It's school night."

"But it's just the second day, so we still don't have any homework," I said. I didn't know about Delta or Enid or the twins, but I did actually have homework. Mr. Rosenberg didn't play around. He gave us homework on the first day of school, and I swear I heard he'd give homework on the last day of school too, even though eighth graders would be going off to a whole other school.

But freedom days weren't just freedom days for us kids. Even Ma seemed to breathe a little deeper on those days when the Daddy didn't come home too early, so I thought I'd test my luck. It worked.

"Eat up all your food," Ma said with a little shrug, then moved on to painting her right hand. Delta leaned over and turned on the television.

"Scooby Doo," I said. Delta gave me a dirty look.

"Oprah," Ma said without looking up from her nails.

One Wednesday afternoon a couple weeks into the school year Rachael pulled me into the bathroom as soon as I got to the community center. We had completed decorating and organizing the day-care center room over the summer, and the day care had officially gone into business a couple weeks earlier. That meant the room had been taken over by whining and drooling toddlers and was no longer our special space. We used Mr. Levinson's office once in a while, and other times we spun wild enough lies to get out of the center altogether and hid out in the back booth of the pizza parlor next door. Rachael always had money for slices and—if we were feeling especially brave or just didn't care about being caught—playing the video games up front. But mostly we used the bathroom for privacy.

Rachael locked the door and turned to face me. Lips pursed, I lunged at her and bumped my nose against her knuckles as she drew her hands over her face.

"No, no, no." Her voice sounded as though it were coming from a tube and echoed weirdly against the tile walls. She slid down to the floor, then removed her hands from her face.

"I have to tell you something," she said as she tugged on my jeans.

I slid down to the floor next to her.

"What'd I do?" I asked.

Rachael shook her head. "It isn't about you. Well, it's about you, but . . ."

"What?" I was getting worried. Rachael had invited me to her Halloween party. Even though Halloween was weeks away, it was going to be such a big-deal party that she'd been planning since over the summer. I absolutely couldn't wait to go. It was going to be the best night of my life. But that was what had me nervous. I couldn't help thinking that maybe she would change her mind about me being at her Halloween party and letting all her cool high school friends know that she was friends with someone like me. I wouldn't be surprised one bit. And it wouldn't be the first time someone had pretended to be my friend for their own laughs. But then I thought, *What about the things we've been doing together? She couldn't have been faking that, could she?*

"Listen, if you don't want me at your party, it's no big deal. I think I might have other plans anyway." *Like what, like what?* "This girl at my school, Suzanne. She's having a party and—"

"Isn't that the girl who's always ignoring you?"

"Well, yeah, she used to, but . . ."

"It's not about my party, Karina."

"Then, what is it, already?"

"Hey, you know what?" she responded with a fake smile. "It's probably not a big deal at all."

"What isn't?"

"It's your dad."

"My stepfather?"

"Yeah, him. See, the thing is I heard my dad talking about how he stopped coming to the parenting class. But maybe it's not a big deal, right? I mean, you said things were better at home, right? So it doesn't matter much."

"I guess not," I said. But there was something else. I could tell by the way she was looking at me as if she was really sorry about something that had just happened to me but was glad it hadn't happened to her. But the Daddy not going to the class anymore? Why would she think that was a big deal? In fact, why wouldn't she think that was great news?

"If he isn't coming to the class, doesn't your dad have to tell the court people?" I asked.

Rachael chewed her top lip and stared at me.

"Doesn't he have to tell?" I asked again. "And then wouldn't they make him go or arrest him or something if he doesn't?"

"He usually gives people a few chances," she said quietly.

I shook my head. "There's something else, Rachael. Tell me."

Rachael took a deep breath. "I've made a decision," she said.

"Tell me," I said again.

"I'm going to tell my dad the truth about your step-dad, Karina. About him beating on you guys and what really happened to Enid."

"There's no way you would do that, Rachael, because you made a promise," I said.

Rachael shook her head. "What's going to happen when he starts in on you guys again? You told me he's starting to smack your little brothers already, didn't you?"

"Just a couple whacks on the butt, that's all," I said. "He didn't even use a belt or a cord."

"Jeez, Karina. You gotta be kidding."

"Anyway, I'd get in trouble. I already let everyone think I beat up Enid."

"You lied 'cause you were scared. They'll understand," said Rachael.

"Yeah, right," I said. "My mom would kill me if she found out I told you. They drag him away, and then she'll have to work a million hours a week, and you know what? She'll just let him back in again eventually, and then I'll really be screwed!"

"There has to be something we can do."

I stood up. "You don't know anything about it, Rachael, so just butt out! If you do stick your nose in it, I swear I'll never talk to you again—ever."

I reached for the door, but Rachael was sitting against it and didn't move. I looked down at her and really wanted to say something more. I wanted to talk and talk and talk until she believed the lie I was trying to make myself believe. Until I completely convinced us both that Tuesdays and Thursdays would forever be freedom days and that the rest of the week the Daddy would do nothing more than curse at us and whack Gerald's and Roland's behinds. Instead I pulled Rachael up off the floor and wrapped my arms around her waist. She threw her arms around my neck. As her elbows dug into my shoulder blades and her nose left a wet spot on my neck, I wondered if butt-kicking angels could have hair that smelled of strawberries and floor wax.

Freedom days ended the following Tuesday. Ma was at work when the Daddy came home early. Even earlier than before he started going to the community center. We were just home from school and still at the dinner table when he walked in. We ate the rest of our dinners in silence. Later we got prepared for things to go back to normal at our house again. I put some coloring books and crayons for Gerald and a pacifier for Roland into the cabinet underneath the sink in the hallway bathroom. Delta went back to sleeping on the floor.

It pissed me off, really. It turned out that it didn't even matter if the Daddy spent lots of time around the house or not, he managed to screw up my life anyway. I didn't think that Rachael would tell. But I didn't like the way it made me feel to know how she probably felt about me now. Like maybe I was responsible for any beat-ups that were coming because I wouldn't tell the truth. Rachael wasn't completely wrong about that, but what I couldn't seem to make her understand was that the beat-ups would come no matter what.

Still, though, it really bummed me out to have Rachael looking at me funny when we were together, like I was a wimp. That's when I came up with the Plan. The Plan was really simple: In order to put off the Daddy's beat-ups for as long as possible, we had to stay away from home as much as possible. It was so simple that I might have thought it up sooner, only until I met Rachael, there wasn't any place for us to be but at home and at school. As much as I didn't want to be at home and dreamed of turning eighteen and leaving, until I met Rachael, there was no one worth running away to. Now I had Rachael and the community center. And with their day-care facility and after-school programs there was no reason why all of us—Enid and Delta, the twins and the babies—couldn't spend afternoons over there. By the time the center closed for the evening, Aunt Merlude would be home and sometimes so would Ma. I told Rachael about the Plan first.

"What about weekends, Karina?" she asked. "Are you all going to spend the rest of your lives in this place?"

I shrugged. "Well, it's a start," I said.

"I only come here a couple days a week, you know," said Rachael.

I shrugged again. "Well, if you come more often, you'll see me more often."

"Hmmm...," she said, smiling. "I'll think about it."

But Enid wasn't so sure about the Plan at first. "How would the twins get there?" she asked. "They'd have to get permission from a parent to ride a different bus after school, and that's even if there is a bus that goes by the community center from their school. And how would we all get home?"

I hadn't thought of all that. I leaned against the sink as Enid washed dishes. Delta had taken the babies into the bathroom for their bath, and the twins had disappeared from the kitchen after cleaning the table and sweeping the floor. I didn't want any of them to know about the Plan until Enid helped me figure out the details. Now I was glad I'd done that, because there were way more details than I had figured.

"And plus, what are we gonna tell Ma?" Enid continued.

"After-school programs," I said. "I don't think she'll mind. She likes Mr. Levinson."

"Yeah, but still . . . ," said Enid. "We have to figure this out better."

I heard a key turn in the front door. "Think of something," I whispered as the Daddy walked up the front stairs, and I took off through the back door and onto the porch.

The next day, before the Daddy came home for dinner, Enid said that we weren't going to throw the leftovers away anymore. Instead she wrapped them tight in four separate pieces of aluminum foil and hid them in the refrigerator.

"Before I leave for school in the morning, I'm going to put two of those dinners in your backpack"—she pointed at me—"and two in yours, Dee Dee."

I knew what Enid was talking about, but Delta didn't.

"But we get free lunch, Fee Fee," she said.

Enid looked at me, and I let her explain to Delta about the Plan.

"I want the both of you to go to the community center every day after school. You can eat the dinners there, but tell Ma that the center people are the ones feeding you, okay?"

We nodded.

"And Katu? Tonight you tell Ma that the center has a new program for kids Jack and Joseph's age, so they won't be getting on the bus after school, okay? And two of these dinners are for them, so make sure they eat."

"I will," I said. "How are you getting to the community center?"

Enid shook her head. "I have to come home after school anyway to watch Roland and Gerald," she said. "There's no way for me to get from here to the center."

"Yeah, but then you'll be the only one here, and Daddy . . ." Delta didn't finish her thought.

"Just don't worry about me, okay?" said Enid, and she looked away from us.

Boy, you have no idea how much I want to tell you that when Delta and I looked at each other that afternoon and realized what Enid was about to do for us, we told her no way and said that we were all in this together and that we'd stick by one another and all that one-for-all-and-all-for-one *After School Special* crap, but I'd be lying. It looked like Enid was about to throw herself in front of the Daddy for us again, and I did nothing about it but stand there and feel my ears burn and wonder why I could never be that strong.

"What if we get caught?" asked Delta.

"You know Ma and Daddy don't have a clue what's going on except for going to work and making sure we eat like cows and beating the shit out of us," said Enid real confidently.

But she had a worried look on her face. Enid took a deep breath and looked at the clock. Less than twenty minutes till the Daddy came home. She pulled me by the arm far down the hallway.

"Katu, the only way this is going to work is if you figure out how to get the four of you back home after the center closes," whispered Enid. "I couldn't figure out that part."

"Uncle Jude . . ."

Enid shook her head. "Even if he's sober enough to do it, Aunt Merlude or Ma might ask how come the program at the center doesn't drop you guys off."

"Well, what about whoever's picking up Jack and Joseph from school?"

"He can't," said Enid. "He'll be at work by then."

I started to think out loud. "I gotta figure a way to get Mr. Levinson or Laurel to take us home every day without telling them exactly why we never go home after school," I said.

Enid nodded. "Plus, you need to come up with something about how Jack and Joseph are getting to the center by themselves."

"Oh God, Enid!"

"You tell great stories, Katu. I'm totally sure you can come up with something good."

I couldn't help but smile. "Okay, I'll think of something," I said.

Then Enid started giggling.

"What?" I asked.

"I was just thinking that whatever you come up with better not be as crazy as the stories you tell Augustin," she said. "I mean, you keep him entertained for hours, and he doesn't even have any idea what you're saying."

"What are you talking about?"

"I'm talking about all those lies you tell him," she said.

"No," I said. "What do you mean he doesn't have any idea what I'm saying?"

Enid stopped giggling. "Katu, please tell me you know Augustin doesn't speak any English."

"He does so speak English," I said. "He talks to me all the time."

"He talks to you? Like, what does he ever say?"

"Stuff," I said, and pouted. Enid just had to be wrong about this. Augustin had basically been my best friend ever since he moved into the house and before I met Rachael. I told him things I didn't tell anyone else. Yeah, sure, sometimes I told him things the way I wished they had happened and not quite *exactly* the way they had happened. But still . . .

"I mean, he answers me when I talk to him," I whined.

"Okay," said Enid, and she started giggling again. "Tonight when he gets home, go down there and tell him something like . . . like, tell him in a real calm voice that there's a snake under his bed and it's crawling toward his chair, and watch what he says."

Enid headed back toward the kitchen. "If that's true, then why didn't you tell me before?" I asked, following her.

"Because once you started talking his ears off, you stopped talking mine off," she said.

"That's not nice," I said as I held a dustpan in place while Joseph swept dirt into it.

"I'm sorry, Katu," said Enid. "I didn't think it mattered to you who was sitting there, as long as someone was there for you to talk at."

"That's so stupid," I said.

Delta turned from the dishes she was washing in the sink and asked Enid, "So you finally told her Augustin doesn't speak English?"

Enid was right about everything. Ma and the Daddy didn't ask questions when we told them about the after-school programs. I was able to come up with a story for Mr. Levinson about why we were at the center every day (Rachael and I needed to help each other with schoolwork; Delta wanted to run a community center one day, so she needed to start practicing right now; and the twins had to be there because Rachael all of a sudden really, really wanted to tutor little Haitian kids in English), plus how the twins got there (Uncle Jude dropped them off during his taxi route and never came in 'cause he was a busy, busy man with a real bad knee) and why we needed a ride home afterward (dinnertime was prime moneymaking time for cabdrivers, and Uncle Jude and Daddy couldn't afford to drop everything and come get us).

And I'd been spending years talking to a guy who didn't speak English. Not a lick of it.

19.

We almost made it through the month of October on the Plan. Almost. Then two nights before Halloween, Mr. Levinson and Rachael and Father Sanon came over to our house. Mr. Levinson was carrying a huge cardboard tube. He popped the plastic top off, pulled out a huge rolled-up sheet, and opened it up on the table.

"Karina, would you get four drinking glasses to hold these corners down for me, please?"

Rachael helped me place the glasses so that the sheet wouldn't curl up. Then Mr. Levinson, Father Sanon, Ma, and Augustin crowded around the table so quickly I had to shove Rachael a little to get a good look. At first I thought what Mr. Levinson had pulled out of the tube was some sort of map, but it wasn't.

The entire sheet was covered by a grid of boxes. The boxes running down the left side were biggest, and in each of them was the word "Republican" or "Democrat" or "Independent." Each box that said Republican also had a picture of an elephant. Each Democrat box had a picture of a donkey. Next to each box on the left was a row of boxes going all the way to the right side of the sheet. Each of those boxes had someone's name written in, and below each name was a picture of something that looked like a toilet flusher.

"This is exactly what it will look like when you go into the voting booth," said Mr. Levinson. "Of course, it won't be this big."

The grown-ups all laughed. Rachael and I looked at each other and rolled our eyes.

"Is this also your first time voting, Jean?" Mr. Levinson asked.

"Oui," Augustin answered.

"It's very easy," said Mr. Levinson. "First, when you walk into the booth, you'll see a big handle in front of you. Pull the handle this way"—Mr. Levinson made a big sweeping motion with his arm—"and the curtain will close behind you."

Ma and Augustin nodded.

"Then all you need to do is find the *cheval*," he said. Ma and Augustin and Father Sanon smiled. Mr. Levinson seemed mighty pleased with himself, but I couldn't help busting his bubble.

"A *cheval* is a horse," I said.

Ma sucked her teeth and pinched my arm.

"Well, my French is a bit rusty. It's been more years than I care to admit since college." Mr. Levinson laughed, and the grown-ups laughed with him.

"What is the word for 'donkey,' Karina?" he asked.

"Bourrique," I said only after looking at Ma and seeing that it was okay to answer.

"And 'elephant'?"

"Éléphant," I answered.

"At least that's an easy one," he said, and led the grown-ups in another round of senseless laughter.

When they'd all calmed down, Mr. Levinson returned to the sheet and said, "Once you find the *bourrique*"—he turned and winked at me—"then you just go across and pull the lever." Mr. Levinson used his finger to trace across the page, stopping to mime pulling the lever under each name in the Democrat rows.

"Once you're finished voting, you pull the big handle back the other way, and the curtain will open up behind you."

"No one can change your vote or even see who you voted for once the curtain opens," said Father Sanon in French.

"Bon," said Augustin.

"Yes," said Mr. Levinson. "Very *bon*."

Rachael and I hightailed it out of the kitchen before any of the adults, doubled over in laughter, could fall on us.

Out in the hallway Rachael was giving me that look again. She had this look where she would smile like she had a big ole secret and she would stare at me, and my stomach would get all nervous. But this time I didn't look away, and I think she got more nervous than I'd ever been. She backed away from me a little. Maybe she thought I was going to try to kiss her right there in the hallway with our parents in the next room.

"Wanna see something in my room?" I asked her.

She looked back toward the kitchen, though we were far enough down the hallway that we couldn't see anyone in there. We could still hear them laughing, of course.

"We've got a bunch more people to show the voting guide to," she said.

"It'll only take a second."

Rachael giggled. "Yeah, I'm sure." I didn't know what she meant by that, but I turned and headed up the stairs, and she followed.

"Do you only teach Haitian people how to vote?" I asked.

"Me and my dad do the Haitian families, Bethel and some other people split up and do the Chinese, and my brother goes with that new guy at the center to talk to the new Vietnamese immigrants," she answered.

"Seth speaks Vietnamese?"

"Yeah, right. That moron can barely speak English. But he picked that one 'cause there's only, like, ten houses to go to, so they get done in two nights," she said. "That way he doesn't have to give up too many precious nights with his stupid girlfriend."

"I like Brandi," I said. "She seems nice."

Rachael shrugged. "Whatever."

I opened the door to my room and found Delta and the twins on the floor playing go fish.

"Get out," I said to them.

"I don't think so, Katu," said Delta. "This is my room too." She was still pissed about the Halloween party that Rachael had invited me to. I hadn't told her yet that Ma said I had to take her. I was pissed about that, so I figured I'd let her suffer awhile before I told her.

"We need a little privacy here, Delta." She ignored me. "I guess I'll just have to tell Ma you're being rude to our guest," I said.

I thought that would get her for sure, because Delta might have been Ma's holy favorite, but I had a whole real-life family who were totally into me and they were rich and they were white. I figured it wouldn't be long before I ended up the favorite daughter, and I wouldn't have to sit through four church services a week to do it.

Instead Delta looked up at me and said, "I guess I'll just have to tell Ma you guys get all the *privacy* you need in the bathroom at the community center."

Then she cocked her head and smiled at me and then at Rachael. Rachael looked like she was about to stroke out. My heart started thudding so hard my chest hurt. Then my head started to spin, and before I could stop myself, I played the one card that would get Delta, no doubt. I let out the one secret Delta had told me and no one else. The secret I had sworn I'd take to my grave.

I said, "Yeah, but not as much *privacy* as you got that time in Mr. Hollings's car."

Delta was so frozen in shock she couldn't even get the dumb smile off her face. But her eyes started to tear. I felt like total crap. I would have taken it back if I could. I mean, it was only me and her and Rachael in the room. Yeah, the twins were there, but I knew they had no clue what Delta meant when she mentioned privacy in the bathroom. I didn't have to bring up Mr. Hollings. I didn't have to go there. But it was too late.

"Who's Mr. Hollings?" asked Rachael calmly. It was

obvious she had sensed that whatever secret I had on Delta was bigger than what Delta had on us.

"No one," I said quickly. "It was just a joke." I tried to catch Delta's eye as she dropped the cards and started pushing the twins toward the door. She wouldn't look at me, but in my mind I was screaming, *I'm sorry! I'm sorry! I'm so sorry, Dee Dee!*

I closed the door as they left and turned back to Rachael.

"I'm gonna show you something, but you have to swear not to tell anyone," I whispered. I think my voice was shaking a little. I still couldn't believe what I had just done to Delta, but I thought if I could pretend it was no big deal, then Rachael wouldn't pry about it.

"I won't tell," said Rachael.

"Cross your heart and hope to die?"

When someone says that, you're supposed to say "Stick a needle in my eye," but Rachael didn't. Instead she leaned in and kissed me. For a second I forgot what I was going to show her. Suddenly she ducked sideways and ran and jumped onto Enid's bed. I nearly fell over.

"Well?" she asked.

"Well what?" I asked.

"I promise I won't tell."

"I wouldn't get in trouble anyway. You're the one who did it to me first."

"Not that, stupid!" Rachael acted like she was annoyed, but then she giggled and held Enid's pillow up to her face. "You said you wanted to show me something," she said into the pillow.

"Oh, yeah."

"Well?" she asked again as she brought the pillow back down to her lap.

I walked over to her and said, "Get up."

I lifted Enid's mattress just enough to stick my hand in. When I dropped the mattress back in its place, Rachael saw what I was holding and said, "Oh . . . my . . . God," all singsongy like. Now it was my turn to giggle. I grabbed her hand and pulled her down to the floor. We sat with our backs up against my bed, facing Enid's bed, and I dropped the magazine I had swiped from Uncle Jude's apartment onto her lap.

"You bought this?" she asked.

"Of course not," I replied. "I borrowed it from my uncle."

"Yeah, sure."

"Well, he doesn't *know* I borrowed it," I clarified.

Slowly Rachael began turning the pages, her mouth hanging open and getting wider with each new naked-lady picture. I had seen them enough to know what was in it, so I just watched Rachael. When she got to the one with Miss America doing what she was doing with the other naked lady, Rachael screamed, and I pinched her leg.

"Sorry," she said. "This is so gross."

"Yeah, I know," I said, and then we both started to laugh.

"This is way ickier than the magazines my brother has," she said.

"He showed them to you?" I asked.

"As if," she said. "I found them underneath the washing machine in the guest bathroom. I keep checking, like, every day, but it's been the same three dirty magazines since last summer."

I just looked at her, and she knew just what I was thinking. "I'll show you when you come to the party," she said.

"I've got bad news about that," I said.

"Don't tell me you're not coming!"

"No, I am," I said. "But my mother says I have to bring Delta, too."

"No biggie," she said.

"Cool."

"Maybe you could come as the first black Miss America."

"As if!" We both said that together and started laughing. I wrapped an arm around Rachael's neck, pulled her to me, and kissed her. I held on as long as I could, but eventually I had to come up for air.

Rachael shook her head and stared at me.

"Why do you always look at me like that?" I asked.

"Because we could do that for more than two seconds at a time if you didn't hold your breath, you know."

"That was at least a minute long," I said.

"Keep dreaming!"

"I just need more practice," I said. "Let me try again."

Rachael leaned and leaned, and when our lips were just about to touch, the bedroom door swung open.

"Time to go with your father, Rachael."

Rachael flung the magazine so hard underneath Enid's bed that I heard it slap up against the wall on the other side. We jumped up off the floor and turned toward the door.

The Daddy stood there blocking the entire doorway. He was looking over our heads toward the other side of Enid's bed. I wondered if he could see the magazine from where he stood, but neither Rachael nor I dared to look back in that direction. After an eternity the Daddy moved away from the doorway.

"Thanks, Mr. Gaston," said Rachael as she walked quickly out of the room, then ran down the stairs.

"You go say good night to Father Sanon," said the Daddy, and as much as I didn't want to leave that magazine in the room with him, I ran out and down the stairs after Rachael.

20.

Delta was dressed up as a princess for Rachael's Halloween party. She wore the white dress Enid had worn to her first Communion. It was so long on her that Augustin had to cut away at the front so Delta could walk without tripping. But he left the back side alone, so it looked like the train of a bride's dress. Rachael and I had snuck out of the center the day before and bought Delta one of those fancy white party masks that have feathers sticking out from the corners and only cover your eyes and nose. She took it, but she didn't say thank you. She hadn't said anything to me since the night I said what I did about her and Mr. Hollings.

Both Jack and Joseph were dressed as Batman. Enid tried to get one of them to switch to Robin, but they said they'd go trick-or-treating only if they wore the same outfit as each other. Gerald sat on the floor looking like a blue blob with metal legs. He was supposed to be a Smurf, but I didn't know which one.

Roland sat in Enid's lap, wrapped in a plain black cloth as Augustin finished tucking red cotton horns into a backward baseball cap Roland was wearing on his head. He was supposed to be a little devil, but he didn't look too evil with his thumb in his mouth.

Enid wasn't wearing a costume. She was taking the boys trick-or-treating, and Augustin said he'd go with her to carry Gerald, since his braces would have to come off when we were all ready to leave.

I sat cross-legged on Augustin's bed, trying to hold off putting on my costume as long as I could. I had wanted to go to Rachael's party as Wonder Woman, but Ma said no when she found out I'd be wearing a bathing suit with tights and nothing else except a rain slicker over my shoulders as a cape. Augustin had a bunch of scraps left from the bridesmaid dresses he'd made over the summer, and Rachael had given me all the green eye shadow she could find in her vanity. So I was going as a lime green Incredible Hulk, and I wasn't happy about it.

Plus, my stomach had been queasy ever since the Daddy walked in on Rachael and me two nights earlier. Not that I wasn't planning on going to Rachael's party, I definitely was, but I didn't know how many more times I'd need to throw up before leaving. After Rachael left that night, I went down to the basement to talk at Augustin 'cause I was afraid to go in my bedroom to see if the magazine was still there. I finally had to go to bed, though, and when I got up there, the magazine was gone. I knew Delta hadn't found it, because I would have been able to tell by the look on her face. I knew Enid hadn't found it, because she would have said something. That meant only one person could have the magazine.

When Augustin finished with Roland, Enid told me to get dressed or I wouldn't be ready and Uncle Jude would leave me behind. He was supposed to swing by while he was working and take me and Delta over to Rachael's party. Ma and Aunt Merlude were both working late. Delta went upstairs to get lipstick out of Ma's bathroom, and Enid followed with Roland to change his diaper.

I was letting Jack and Joseph smear the green eye shadow all over my face and neck and arms when the Daddy opened the door at the top of the basement stairs and yelled for me to come up.

"Come join me in your room," he said in Creole as I stepped into the hallway.

This was it, I thought. He'd waited until the night he knew I'd be excited about the party to come home early and beat the life out of me because of Rachael and the magazine. It had been months since I'd gotten a beat-up from the Daddy, and I should have been close to wetting myself trying to come up with something to get out of it, or I should have been fainting all over the place, but instead all I could think of, standing in the hallway holding that stupid green costume and biting my lip, was that I hoped the Daddy wouldn't hurt me so badly that I couldn't make it to Rachael's party afterward.

As I squeezed past the Daddy and turned toward the stairs, Enid came down with Roland in her arms, and I stepped to the side to let her down.

"What did you do here?" yelled the Daddy. "What is Ti Wo Wo wearing?"

"It's just a costume," said Enid.

"*KA-TOOM? KA-TOOM!*" the Daddy tried to say in English. "You call my son the devil and say it's a *KA-TOOM?*"

I backed up the stairs slowly.

The Daddy grabbed Roland, then punched Enid in the face once and put Roland down on the floor. As the Daddy bent over and began tearing off Roland's costume, Enid, holding her cheek with both hands, looked for an escape. Angled the way he was in the hallway, the Daddy had her boxed in so she couldn't make a run for it down the hall and into the kitchen or basement and couldn't head up the stairs. Slowly Enid slid along the wall, heading toward the steps that led down to the front door.

"Where are you going?" asked the Daddy as he pushed Roland away with one hand and lunged after Enid with the other. Roland fell onto all fours and, wailing at the top of his lungs, crawled toward the hallway bathroom.

Enid shrieked and took a giant leap down the front stairs. "No more! Please, I can't!" yelled Enid. The Daddy, breathing hard, stumbled after her as she fumbled with the front door. I started following them out, but the Daddy stopped as Enid crossed the driveway and headed toward the back of the house.

"I'll be waiting for you," the Daddy yelled after Enid.

Then he turned to me, pointed up the stairs, and said, "Now!"

I don't know where he'd been hiding it, maybe in

one of his giant pockets, but as soon as we got to my room, the Daddy held the magazine out toward me and asked, "Do you know where people like you go?"

"No, Daddy."

"God puts them in hell," he said. "But before they die and go to hell, God makes their families live in hell on earth."

I said nothing. I didn't know where this hell on earth was, but I thought I had a pretty good idea.

"Are you trying to put me in hell?" asked the Daddy. "Are you trying to make my family live in shame?"

I shook my head, and the Daddy slapped me hard. I fell to my bed.

"What do you think your mother will say when I tell her what kind of friend you are with that white girl?" he asked.

"I don't know," I whispered. I was still holding my face, trying to squeeze the sting out of my cheek, so Daddy aimed his next smack at the side of my head. I heard a hollow popping sound in my ear, then he walked out of the room.

I heard the Daddy go into his room and open the closet door. You could always tell when the Daddy yanked open his closet, because the belts hanging on the inside would slap up against the door. I sat still, waiting for him to come back in my room.

What? You think I should have run like Enid did? It wouldn't have done any good. We'd all done it before, and all that did was stretch one beat-up over the course of several hours, or like the time I actually hid in the shed overnight, over the course of two days. The Daddy would get the beat-ups done no matter how much we tried to stall. It was better just to get it all over with, like yanking a Band-Aid off your arm real quick instead of trying to peel it off slowly.

But as I waited there, I suddenly heard the loudest, the scariest, the most high-pitched scream I've heard in my life, ever, ever, ever. It was so loud that the ear the Daddy had just smacked popped again. I jumped up off the bed, but I was too scared to go any farther. I stood in the middle of my room, and along with the screaming there came loud smacking sounds and finally a huge thump. Then the screaming stopped.

I waited for what seemed like forever, but I didn't hear the Daddy coming back for me, so I took a deep breath, opened the door, and stepped out into the hallway. Delta was standing in the middle of Ma and the Daddy's bedroom with her party mask on her head and her hands covering her mouth, staring at the closet. I walked in.

The Daddy was in a heap on the floor, half in and half out of the closet. There was blood everywhere—gushing out of his Afro and pooling around his head, splattered on his ties and belts on the closet door, dripping down from the clothes on the hangers. He wasn't moving.

Enid stood on the far side of the room hyperventilating and shaking. The punch the Daddy had given her was already swelling up into the shape of two knuckles. On the bruise was a smear of blood with a tear slicing right through it. Blood covered the front of her shirt and down to the knees of her jeans. She had both hands wrapped tightly around a thick wooden slat from the old porch.

"I just couldn't let it happen again," said Enid, staring at the Daddy. Her voice came out in a high-pitched, scratchy hiss, as if someone had wrapped their hands around her neck.

"What are we going to do?" Delta whispered.

I started to shrug, but then I stopped. I looked at the Daddy and then back at Delta and then Enid, and suddenly I did know exactly what to do. I remembered what Rachael had told me about when her dad woke up in the hospital after his heart attack and everything in the world seemed crystal clear to him. He knew he wanted to change his life, and he knew just how to do it. That's how I felt that night standing in Ma's room watching the Daddy bleed. I knew that what Mr. Levinson felt he had to do with his life didn't end up making everyone happy, but I'd also finally decided that maybe sometimes doing something really bad could make even worse stuff not happen to people you loved.

I wanted Enid to have a normal life with a boyfriend and a spot on the softball team, instead of spending all day taking care of six kids and dodging the Daddy's fists. I wanted Delta to go away to college, not come home every day to learn how to be a good housecleaning wife. I wanted Ma to stop being so ashamed of having to make herself live with the Daddy forever because she wasn't educated enough to get a good sit-down job. And to make all that happen, I had to come up with the most important story I'd ever have to tell.

If it didn't work, it would mean no more kissing Rachael and smelling her hair, no more sleepovers and knish dinners, no more being with her and feeling like someone could really like weird ole me. It would mean maybe never seeing Rachael again. It would mean remembering how nice these past few months with her had been from inside a jail cell.

I walked over to Enid, took the wooden slat out of her hands, and placed it on the bed.

"Look at me, Fee Fee," I said. Her eyes floated around the room before meeting mine. "You were never here tonight, okay? You went on a date with Mickey this afternoon as soon as Delta and I came home from school."

Enid shook her head and started backing away from me. The sound of a car pulling into the driveway made us look toward the window.

"Uncle Jude!" said Delta.

I grabbed Enid's arm and pulled her toward me. "Trust me, Enid," I said.

Still hanging on to her arm, I pulled her out of the room and into the hallway. Delta followed us. I grabbed my Incredible Hulk costume off the bed in my room and put it in Enid's hand.

"Rinse your face and put this over your clothes. Then go down to the convenience store and call Mickey to come pick you up," I said.

Enid was still looking like she wasn't too sure. I

grabbed her and hugged her tight and whispered, "And don't come back."

I didn't wait for her to respond. Instead I pushed her toward the stairs while I spoke to Delta.

"You know where the extra car keys are in the kitchen?" Delta nodded. "Tell Augustin and Uncle Jude to come up here. Then get the twins and the babies in the taxi and wait for me," I said.

Delta ran down the stairs, and I returned to Ma's room. I walked over to the Daddy's nightstand, pulled out a handful of cigarettes from an open pack, threw a couple of them on the bed, then laid the rest across the ashtray. When I turned to look around the room for matches, I saw the Daddy's arm twitch and heard him make strangled-sounding gurgles.

As I picked up the wooden slat and quickly straddled the Daddy's body, I heard Augustin and Uncle Jude making their way up the stairs. I raised the slat above my head and popped my hip like a hula dancer, and as I brought it down with all my might, I thought, *Lemongrass and honey. That's what the hair of angels smells like.*

21.

The county newspaper called me a hero. My picture was on the front page. Did you see it? That old, dorky picture of me was from the sixth grade, but you could still tell it was me. The lady who interviewed me and wrote the article was a real good writer, and when people read about how my stepfather fell asleep in bed while smoking a cigarette and I rescued my brothers and sister and cousins just before the house came crashing down, and drove us to the police station, they started sending money to the newspaper for us so that we wouldn't have to live in a homeless shelter. They sent so much money that the newspaper people opened up a special account for Ma at a bank.

The newspaper lady asked me how I'd learned to drive, and I told her that I had spent a lot of time watching Gaston. She didn't look like she really believed that all the way, so I told her that on the night of the fire I had accidentally smacked the car into the side of the house first before backing up and pulling out of the driveway. That way I didn't come off sounding like an expert driver and have to explain that I'd been driving since I was ten. Besides, it was true.

I was so nervous when I got behind the wheel of the car that night that I put the car in drive instead of reverse. Delta, who was sitting real calmly in the front passenger seat, told me that the crunching sound I'd heard before I smacked into the garage door was Gerald's leg braces. She'd taken them off and left them on the driveway so that Gerald wouldn't be too heavy to lift into the car. Then she did something that really distracted me. As I tried to get the car into reverse, she rolled down the window, yanked off her necklace and cross, and flung them out onto the driveway, then pulled the party mask down over her face. She didn't say any prayers out loud that night. I don't think she said any quietly, either.

The newspaper lady got something else wrong too. I didn't head straight to the police station that night. Instead Uncle Jude had me drive to his apartment complex and wait there for him. When his taxi arrived a few minutes later, Augustin got out of the passenger side carrying two suitcases and started across the parking lot toward the building. I got out of the car and ran to Uncle Jude. He grabbed me around the waist.

I buried my head in his chest and said, "Thank you, Uncle Jude." He smelled like burning paper and sweat and his shirtsleeves were smeared with blood.

I pulled away from him to talk to Augustin, but he was nowhere in the parking lot. From the front door of the building a little boy came out wearing a Mets baseball uniform and carrying an orange trick-or-treat lantern. Augustin had disappeared.

Uncle Jude walked over to the Daddy's taxi and leaned in. He looked at the princess in the passenger seat, then at the two Batmans, the Smurf, and the little devil.

"When are we going to get candy?" I heard Gerald ask.

"I bring later," said Uncle Jude. "Candy for every-body."

Uncle Jude stepped away from the car and looked in the direction of our house. I looked with him. Though the sun had completely set by then, we saw the clouds of grayish black smoke as soon as they appeared above the trees.

Uncle Jude turned to me, rubbed my shoulders, and said, "It's time now, my sweetheart. Go to police."

We lived at the Holiday Inn the whole time we were having the new house built. Delta and I had our own room. The twins were in a room with Aunt Merlude, and Ma had a room for her and Gerald and Roland. At first Ma cried a lot about Enid. Delta had to tell her over and over that Enid didn't get stuck in the burning house that night. I wrote a letter to the high school principal saying that because of the awful tragedy Enid had been sent back to Haiti to live with her real father. Then I made Ma sign it.

No one asked about Augustin, of course. It wasn't like we had a sign hanging on the house, with an arrow pointing to the basement, that said AUGUSTIN LIVES HERE. Delta and I tried to figure out where he'd gone, but we weren't really worried about him. He had already proved he could come back from the dead. And besides, deep down I have this feeling that if we ever need him, he'll show up.

I went back to school a few days after Gaston's funeral. For almost a whole week the kids looked at me different. They smiled and pointed a lot, but not like they were making fun of me as usual. They didn't throw things. Instead some of them would sorta half wave—you know, like what you do to popular kids when you're not real sure if they'll let you talk to them? It totally weirded me out. Even Suzanne came over to me in the hallway on my first day back and said, "Oh, Karina, are you okay?" while she patted me on the arm. David stopped by and said, "I didn't know you could drive, Karina. Cool." And Mrs. M. kept breaking out in these bony-faced smiles every time she saw me.

But then one day when I was using the whole awful tragedy as my ticket out of gym class for the second time that week, I ran into Gorilla Arms on my way to lie down in the nurse's office. The halls were empty, and stupid me, thinking *everyone* was treating me like a hero now, I didn't turn and run. Jeffrey took two big hops like a damn kangaroo and landed right in my face. He took me by the upper arm and pushed me into the lockers. I bit down on my lip.

"Do you want me to be your daddy now?" he asked, leaning into me.

"Sure," I said. "Then I can do to you what I did to him."

I heard Jeffrey's breath catch for a second and felt his grip on my arm loosen. He was going to call my bluff, though. I felt that, too. I'd only caught him off guard for a second. But that second was all I needed. I brought my knee up fast and hard and clocked him right in the balls. I jumped over him when he dropped to the floor, and took off for the nurse's office.

After that Gorilla Arms didn't bother me anymore. And neither did his retard friends. Even the rest of the kids in school stopped treating me like a movie star they were afraid to ask for an autograph and more like . . . well, more like the crazy bully you didn't want to make eye contact with or end up alone with in the hallway between classes. That sucked. But to tell you the truth, it didn't suck anywhere near as bad as being pounded on every day.

Then a couple weeks before Christmas, Rachael and Laurel and Mr. Levinson showed up at our hotel room. Rachael handed me a big yellow manila envelope. It was addressed to "Karina Lamond," but the street address was the community center. I held the envelope in my hand and stared at the Levinsons until they got the hint. Mr. Levinson said that maybe they should go say hello to my mom, and then the three of them left.

Delta sat next to me on my bed as I opened the envelope. Inside the big envelope were four smaller envelopes. One said "Katu," another said "Dee Dee," and a third one said "To Whom It May Concern." The fourth envelope said "open first" and was the kind of envelope you use for birthday cards and stuff.

It was filled with naked Polaroid pictures of Enid. Enid's back, Enid's front, Enid's legs and arms and face. They were pictures of that last beat-up Enid got. There was an index card with the pictures. Enid had written a note to me that said I shouldn't open the "To Whom It May Concern" letter, only keep it safe along with the pictures. "I know you'll know when to use them if you need to," she wrote. "I trust you."

I looked over at Delta to see if she was okay, and she was staring at me.

"*Fromage,*" she said as I stuffed the pictures back into the envelope, then handed her the one with her name on it.

I opened my envelope, and there was a letter about four pages long in more of Enid's awful handwriting. Most of the stuff she wrote to me was pretty personal. I'll let her tell you about it if she wants to. But there was a part where she explained why she was so mad at Ma and why she didn't want to talk to her. I understood how she felt, but I right away hoped that one day they could be like mother and daughter again.

"Open yours," I said to Delta. She had been holding on to her envelope and watching me read my letter.

"There's something in here," she said.

I patted the envelope and felt something hard. Delta began opening the envelope real carefully, like she wanted it to stay looking new. When she finally had it unsealed, she turned it upside down on the bed. A letter that looked just like mine fell out, and so did a tiny little packet wrapped in notebook paper and taped closed. Delta picked up the packet and opened it. Inside was her necklace and cross. She started to cry.

I didn't think Delta would mind, so I picked up her letter and read it to her. In the PS part Enid wrote, "God helps those who help themselves."

Delta actually stopped crying and started to laugh.

"What?" I asked.

"That's probably the most religious saying she knows."

I laughed too.

Then there was a PPS part in each of our letters. There Enid wrote, "You were both right. We can be guardian angels for one another."

Delta put on her necklace and kissed her cross.

22.

I wish Ma was here at the wedding today, Mickey. Maybe after you and Enid are married, you can start working her on the Ma issue, see if she'll be able to forgive her someday. I totally understand Enid being upset because Ma could've stopped things before they got so out of hand with Gaston. But you know, as brave as Uncle Jude and Augustin were that night, they could've done something sooner, too, and I know Enid is not upset with them. I guess sometimes the right thing is so hard to do that people won't do it until they have absolutely no other choice. But Ma always wanted the best for us, even if sometimes the way she showed it seemed pretty warped.

I've written plenty of letters to Enid, but you tell her too. Ma is not so bad anymore. She doesn't hit us. She whines a little more, and I have to admit that the guilt trips she lays on now are sometimes worse than before, but we can tell she's trying. And she's home more now too. No more overnights at the factory, no more working on the weekends.

After Enid's first letter came, I went over to the community center and had a little chitchat with Mr.

Levinson and Father Sanon. I brought the pictures with me but not the "To Whom It May Concern" letter. I still haven't opened that yet.

Ma works at the community center now and not the bottling factory. She does basically the same stuff I used to do when I volunteered there, but she gets paid. Can you believe it? Ma has a sit-behind-a-desk job. Her head was a little big about it for a few weeks, but we didn't mind. Especially not Delta, who told Ma that she wanted to be the sit-behind-a-desk boss of the people with sit-behind-a-desk jobs, only she couldn't go to just community college if she wanted that to come true, and Ma said okay. If Delta gets into Harvard, she can go.

Delta skipped another grade the year after the fire, so now we're both in tenth grade. You know what that means, right? I'll be visiting up here a lot. I know I can crash with you and Enid, right?

Delta says I should try to get into college, and Mrs. Mahajan agrees. She told me at the end of eighth grade that the counselors couldn't have put me in special-education classes just because of homework and my rotten attitude because my standardized test scores were so high. She said that she'd told me about special ed only because she knew I had potential and wanted to scare some sense into me before I got left back and lost hope and dropped out of school and became a statistic or something. Great trick, right? Not. Anyway, the joke was on Mrs. M. I was already a statistic.

Delta wants me to go to college somewhere around

here in Boston, so that way all the girls will be together. She says my being a hero and all the volunteer work I do at the community center will look so good on a college application that maybe they'll give me a break about my grades. They're not quite as bad as they used to be, but they're still pretty lousy.

I'm not so sure about leaving Chestnut Valley just yet, though. Ma could use my help with Gerald and Roland. Plus, I want to be a writer and I'm already a pretty good storyteller, so I don't know what four more years of homework would accomplish. Maybe I'll just take a couple of writing classes at the community college and drive the taxi around the county in the afternoon to make some money. After Gaston died, Uncle Jude renamed the company Jude's Red Limo Co. and painted that on both taxis. He lets Ma use one as her regular car. Oh yeah, Ma can drive now. Uncle Jude taught her. And he even let me show her how to parallel park, once I could do it without hitting anything.

Stop laughing at me. Jack and Joseph told me about *your* wonderful driving skills, flying down the highway a hundred miles an hour to get them to the community center after school. At least I go the speed limit. Don't worry. I do it legally. I have my learner's permit now.

Besides, Rachael is thinking about going to Columbia, and if she does, she said that I can drive into the city and visit her whenever I want, because New York City is the place to be if you're a writer. Well, actually she said I can visit her only if I go to the doctor and have them fix my fainting spells. I've been passing out a lot less since Gaston died, but a few weeks ago it happened in Rachael's car when she was driving us to a movie. She totally freaked out and started yelling about what if it had happened while *I* was driving and I went and got myself killed and then what would she do? So she told her dad. He took me to a hospital, and they stuck me into a giant tube and took pictures of my brain. I don't know yet what they found out, but I kept telling them I felt just fine.

Anyway, maybe you should go on up front near the minister now. They'll be starting "Here Comes the Bride" in a few minutes. I need to find Gerald and Roland. Last I saw them, they were outside making snow angels after Delta and I had gotten them all dressed. Delta started to get upset with them, but I told her that it's okay because Gerald and Roland are angels in training. Angels will be all around us now. Like me and Delta and Uncle Jude and Augustin. We'll make sure absolutely no one hurts Enid, or her kids when she has some.

But you plan on treating Enid right, don't you? Then, don't look so worried, Mickey.

We're all perfect angels.

A NOTE FROM THE AUTHOR

—

Nobody's life is simple. Certainly, Karina's isn't. In telling the story of the Lamond sisters getting tired of being kicked around and finding the courage to fight back, Karina reveals, almost casually, that one of her sisters suffers from bulimia, the other has been molested, and she herself experiences fainting spells due to head trauma. These aren't inconsequential issues, and I know that most kids won't be able to relate to them directly, yet I didn't feel the need to have Karina make extensive comments about them. This is because no one's life is one-dimensional, and savvy young readers know this is true for themselves as well as fictional characters. What is wonderful about writing for young people is that no matter how far their experiences are from those of these girls, they always bring with them their own complex emotions, hectic lives, and complicated worlds— and, when trusted to do so, can relate to just about anything.